HARD T

Stevie was a committed career girl, a feminist to the core—and that maddening James Reid wasn't helping a bit! She *was not* going to weaken herself by falling in love with him. But with a man like James that was easier said than done. Yet, whether Stevie gave in or not—had she any guarantee that James felt the same way about her?

HARD TO HANDLE

BY

JESSICA AYRE

MILLS & BOON LIMITED
15–16 BROOK'S MEWS
LONDON· W1A 1DR

First published 1983
Australian copyright 1983
Philippine copyright 1983
This edition 1983

© Jessica Ayre 1983

ISBN 0 263 74312 8

Set in Monophoto Times 10 on 10½ pt.
01–0883 – 58495

Made and printed in Great Britain by
Richard Clay (The Chaucer Press) Ltd,
Bungay Suffolk

CHAPTER ONE

STEVIE was seized with momentary trepidation as she pressed the large brass doorbell of the mews terrace. Her boss's words echoed in her ears, 'Today's the day, Stevie.' There had been a humorous glint in his eyes as he said it. But in the barrage of instructions which followed, she hadn't had a chance to question him. It was only now, while she stood waiting for some response to her ring, that his manner struck her as peculiar—as if he were setting some kind of trap for her or playing a practical joke.

The door swung open and put an abrupt end to her speculations. A tall, broad-shouldered form filled its frame. As her eyes grew accustomed to the dimmer light of the interior, she made out a roughly hewn face under a crop of bristling dark hair. Two steely eyes looked out at her, examining her coldly but without acknowledging her presence. Stevie's first impulse was to laugh. The man, with his rugged composure, looked like something out of an ad for hunting equipment, or better still, Marlboro country. Larger than life, but not of it.

She stilled the rising laughter and said briskly, 'I'm from the agency.'

His voice growled out of him, 'You change through there. Make it quick!'

'But I . . .' Stevie protested.

'But nothing . . . Just hurry it up. We've a lot of work to do.' His voice willed her through the changing-room door.

Stevie forced herself to turn and face him. 'I'm here to see James Reid,' she said emphatically. 'Where is he?'

'Who the hell do you think I am? Genghis Khan?' he boomed. Stevie thought she detected the glimmer of a twinkle in his eye as he pulled the changing-room door

5

shut behind her, but she couldn't be sure.

'Genghis Khan it is!' she shouted after him defiantly.

'Just get some make-up on, young lady. And make yourself look right!' His tone was almost surly.

'Rude devil!' Stevie thought, her temper rising, and was about to protest again. But she stopped herself. What was the use? She would follow instructions for the time being. After all, there was little point in alienating her first client, her very own first client, before he'd even discovered who she was. She chuckled as she imagined the look on his face when he finally found out that she was not one of his models. Meanwhile she would play the game.

She looked round the room. One wall was completely covered by a mirror. Next to it was a clothes rail, each of its outlandish items neatly labelled; and next to that a dressing table replete with make-up. Some fashion photographer, she thought—not even an assistant or a dresser to help out!

She shrugged and walked over to the clothes rail. The first hanger had a number one printed on it, so opting for logic she lifted the garment off the rail. 'Ridiculous!' she murmured, as she examined the stiffly shiny black pantaloons and the black shirt with flowing sleeves and plunging neckline which went with it. 'What sensible woman would spend money on that?' But dutifully she pulled off her comfortable khaki trousers and the matching military-style jacket and changed into 'item number one', as she called it to herself.

She wound the wide black belt around her waist and glanced at her reflection in a mirror surrounded by bulbs. A smile came to her lips. Yes, as her sister kept insisting, she could easily have been a model, with her long legs, her heavy honey-gold hair, the wide ingenuous green eyes. Perhaps she looked just a trifle too healthy.

Stevie threw a contemptuous sneer at her image. *That* was not what interested her. She had always been what people conventionally called beautiful; there was nothing she could do about it. And it irked her, the way most of them seemed to think it was enough, as if the fact of being beautiful constituted the whole of a person, a way of life. She read it in their glances, which kept returning to her, flattering, envious, or simply surprised. She energetically brushed the thick length of her hair, dabbed some pink on to her cheeks and traced the line of her eyes with a soft grey-green pencil, tricks of the trade she had learnt from her sister.

She could say that much for Genghis Khan—he hadn't responded to her looks one way or another. But then, as a fashion photographer, he was of course used to that special breed: 'beautiful' women. She giggled a little tremulously as she thought again of his face when she finally revealed to him who, in fact, she was.

She made her way towards what she imagined must be the studio. The first door led her into a cupboard, but her second instinct was right, the door opened on to a long room filled with brightly coloured free-standing geometric shapes. Like walking into a contemporary sculpture gallery, Stevie thought. Man-sized cubes, triangles, rectangles stood at odd places in the room. Genghis Khan appeared behind an isosceles. 'The man's a loony,' Stevie reflected, but she smiled at him sweetly.

He looked at her critically for a moment and then gestured her towards a luminous red triangle and switched on two glaring spotlights. As Stevie walked past him, he put out a hand to stop her and moved to adjust the line of her shirt.

'Whoa there, Genghis!' she drew away from his firm touch. 'Just tell me what you want and I'll do it. But hands off!'

He grimaced at her. 'God, they've sent me one of the temperamental ones again!'

Stevie felt like slapping him hard, but she continued to smile sweetly. 'Yes, I guess they have.' Her voice was flippant.

'Right, drape yourself round that triangle,' he ordered.

'Don't think I fancy it,' Stevie muttered under her breath, but she did her best, leaning back against the shape and stretching her arms round it, high over her head. She thought she must look ludicrous.

His groan, as he adjusted his camera echoed her feelings. 'Damn you, woman—move, do something with yourself!'

'Uh—uh, no swearing, there's a lady present,' Stevie chided.

'Move,' he grunted. 'Make yourself part of that shape.'

Stevie did her best as the camera started its clicks in sharp staccato succession. Suddenly James was close to her, holding her eyes, his voice threatening. 'I want you in turn to provide a contrast to that rigid shape and to be as rigid as it is. Understand?'

'Tough bastard, aren't you?' The words were out before Stevie could stop them, and she paled as she met the thrust of his eyes.

A smile flickered over his face. 'Careful, woman, there's a gentleman present!' The smile was gone as soon as it had come. Stevie felt she must have imagined it. He was now concentrating on her as if she were a lifeless object. Then he pushed a hand through her thick hair, forcing it away from her face. She arched away from him, her skin tingling.

The half-smile came back. 'Play with your hair, woman. For the camera.' He emphasised his words by placing the camera in front of his eye.

Stevie had had enough of this game and she went about her gestures half-heartedly, wondering why she was putting up with any of this at all. Oh yes, she remembered; the sight of his astonishment when she finally announced who she was. She would do it now.

'Mr Reid,' she called out, 'I'm not . . .'

The doorbell interrupted her words.

'Damn,' he muttered. 'Why the bell always goes non-stop when my assistant is away, I'll never know.' He walked rapidly out of the studio and Stevie breathed her relief.

'It's probably his model,' she chuckled to herself, waiting impatiently for his embarrassment when he returned.

But when he came back, he was scowling; his manner seethed with impatience. All he said was, 'Let's go,' as once again he aimed his camera at her.

Stevie was taken aback. She was certain that the doorbell had announced the model he was waiting for. He just wouldn't acknowledge his mistake. Her rage gave her the courage to confront him.

'Mr Reid,' she walked deliberately towards him, 'that was your model, wasn't it?'

'*One* of my models,' he grunted, the camera still hiding his face.

'I,' Stevie stressed, 'am *not* one of your models. I'm Stevie Henderson, from the photographic agency, Donne and Brewster.'

At last he lowered the camera from his face. Silence enveloped them both for what seemed an endless moment. Stevie could see the emotions flickering over his face, the anger which finally settled there covered only by a thin veneer of politeness.

'Well, Ms—I take it—Henderson,' he emphasised the ungainly syllable sardonically, 'if you will hide behind a man's name, there are bound to be mistakes.'

'People do usually wait for an introduction before forcing me into a changing room,' Stevie uttered coolly. She wanted some form of apology, never mind the fact that he was her first client. Undoubtedly, he wouldn't be that for long.

'Yes, yes,' he muttered. 'It's a hectic day, what with my assistant off, no dresser, and a tight schedule to keep to.'

Stevie realised this was all she would get out of him, and she was unsure what the next step should be.

He was looking her up and down critically, and suddenly he shook his head. 'Still, I should have known you weren't a model. You're far too combative.'

Before she could take him up on that, a tall, slender woman walked into the studio, her long black hair swinging seductively over bare shoulders.

'Why don't you sit over there, Ms Henderson?' James Reid pointed Stevie towards a stool at the other end of the room. 'Perhaps we can talk after I've finished this session.' His tone was almost gracious.

Stevie recognised that she had been dismissed and she walked quietly towards the designated chair and watched him at work. He was hardly the client she had been led to expect by Mr Brewster. Her boss had simply told her that she was to meet a photographer who was attempting to break into the fashion and advertising world. She had assumed that since she had been assigned to interview him and look at his work, he was youthful potential: like her, someone newly on the scene, who had yet to prove himself. But James Reid was older than she had anticipated, thirty-two at least from the look of him; and he had the authority of someone long in the trade.

She watched him now, totally absorbed in his task, as he put the model through her paces. An energy seemed to flow from him which emitted soundless signals as to how the model should move and drew them both into an electric field separate from the rest of the room. It was almost like watching a ballet. Stevie smiled wryly to herself: that particular harmony had certainly not existed while he had been photographing her. She was obviously not an ideal model. 'Too combative,' he had said, and she congratulated herself on the fact. Yet she felt a glimmer of envy at the twosome's absorption which made her presence so redundant.

When the doorbell rang again, she heard James Reid curse under his breath. He gestured at Stevie, silently ordering her to answer. With a rueful look, she found herself obeying his command. It was a tall, willowy blonde this time, her delicately featured face almost lost in a cloud of hair. She looked at Stevie with surprise. 'Are you replacing Claude?' she asked almost accusingly in heavily-accented tones which Stevie couldn't place.

Stevie shook her head, 'No, I'm James Reid's agent. I'm just answering the door for him.'

'I see,' she said a little suspiciously, and then thrust a hand out at her. 'I'm Irena.'

'Stevie Henderson,' Stevie replied, taking the proffered hand.

The girl nodded and briskly made her way towards the changing room.

Stevie shrugged. Irena was obviously a regular here and didn't like the idea of a new face. Stevie made her way quietly back into the studio and perched on her stool. James Reid didn't acknowledge her return. But when Irena walked into the room, the rhythm of the session changed. He looked up from his camera and Irena came to plant a languorous kiss on his lips. He brushed her away, almost rudely, and without hearing the words they exchanged, Stevie could see that the girl looked crestfallen.

Genghis Khan strikes again, Stevie thought to herself, feeling sorry for the girl and angry at James Reid. She had heard legendary stories of how badly photographers treated their models, but had always sanely assumed that all that was myth. Yet here was James Reid, living it all out in front of her eyes. She wanted to get up and shake him hard, but she controlled the impulse, reminding herself that she was here as a professional, visiting a client.

The tempo of the scene in front of her changed now. Stevie watched James Reid choreograph the girls so that they provided increasingly striking contrasts to one another: the brunette against the blonde, simple black against dazzling cubist patterns, all played in and through the background of the geometric shapes. She found herself eager to see the prints he would produce. They might just be good.

Another model arrived. Stevie dutifully opened the door and ushered her in. Irena and the dark girl changed clothes. The panoply of fashion continued. James Reid kept arranging his models, reloading various cameras, clicking away. At last Stevie began to think he had forgotten her altogether. The afternoon was almost at an end and he had made no sign as to when they were to talk. As he paused momentarily to reload, Stevie rose to interrupt and stake a claim on his time.

'Will there be a chance for us to meet today, Mr Reid?' she asked, her voice cool but insistent.

He looked at her, surprised, as if he no longer remembered who she was and was amazed at her daring to intrude. She met his eyes evenly, challenging him to be rude.

He glanced down at his watch. 'Oh, I have kept you waiting, haven't I?' He seemed more pleased than apologetic.

Stevie wouldn't let him get away with it. 'On the contrary, I've enjoyed myself enormously. I look forward to seeing the prints.'

He nodded, but still made no move to answer her first question.

'Perhaps it would be best if we arranged a specific meeting for tomorrow,' Stevie offered. 'Now that you know I'm not one of your models, we might waste less time.'

A sardonic light flashed through his dark eyes. 'You never can tell. The prints might be encouraging. We could try again . . .'

Stevie felt a flush rising to her cheeks. 'Mr Reid, I have no intention of being put through those paces again. And if you want Donne and Brewster to handle your work, you'd better ring the office and make an appointment to see someone else. At a designated time,' she added, and then, amazed at her own audacity, headed for the door.

'Five o'clock tomorrow afternoon,' she heard him call after her, and as she slammed the studio door behind her, he laughed dryly. 'Ms Henderson, unless you've fallen in love with that garment, you might just leave it behind.'

Stevie stopped in her tracks. She had forgotten she was still wearing the modelling clothes. She stormed into the changing room, stripped off the ensemble and was sorely tempted to fling it at the mirror. Keep cool, Stevie, her inner voice counselled. She hung the clothes on the rail and pulled on her own with angry movements. A look at her watch told her it was almost five o'clock now. Of course! If she had waited just a little, James Reid would have seen her today. But that was the last thing she wanted in her present frame of mind. She finished dressing quickly, unwilling to meet any of the models, and hurried from the house. Closing the door quietly behind her, she broke into a run, and didn't stop for breath until she was well away from the cobbled mews lane.

As she reached the Embankment, her natural good humour took over. Looking down into the murky grey of the Thames, she burst into laughter. Fine spectacle I've made of myself for my first client! she told the fast-moving waters. But then he's hardly a model of good behaviour, is he? She swung her bag over her shoulder and grimaced. She would try to do better tomorrow. Not that that surly Genghis Khan deserved it. No wonder she had had the impression that Mr Brewster was sending her into a trap! Well, she wouldn't give him the pleasure of returning to the office defeated.

With her usual long-legged strides, Stevie made her way towards Westminster. From there she could catch a bus home. There wasn't much point in going back to the office this late, and in any case, she was dying to tell Marissa of her day's adventure.

The sight of the gothic spires in the distance gave her a little thrill. She remembered how, as a small girl, she had thought the Houses of Parliament were a ghostly castle, peopled by wraiths. She chuckled. London continued to excite her: a foreign city full of marvels, yet still, oddly, home. Yes, that was the truth of it. She would never feel quite at home again in the small New England town where she had spent most of her life and where she had always assumed she would return. But equally, she would never be altogether English.

She leapt on to a number 24 bus just as it was pulling away from a stop and clambered up the stairs to the top deck. Miraculously, there was a spare seat and she seated herself gratefully into it. It would be a slow ride back. She watched the sea of cars beneath her, the grandness of Trafalgar Square give way to the bookshops of Charing Cross Road, and then the tawdry bleakness of Camden Town, broken at its northernmost tip by the bright façades of trendy boutiques. At last the bus drew up to its final stop— Hampstead Heath. Stevie walked down the stairs, waving goodbye to the conductor.

After all, this part of London was not so very different from her New England town. She had been living here for a mere six months and already it was hard to walk more than a few hundred yards without greeting a familiar face. She popped into the tearooms which stayed open late to buy some bread and then, on impulse, decided to stop at the local Indian restaurant and get a take-away.

Balancing her packages, she meandered up the hill which bordered the Heath. She loved this road, with its tall willows swaying lazily in the evening breeze. It was just a short walk up to the street where she shared a flat with her sister at the top of a comfortable Victorian house.

Stevie's sister, Marissa, had insisted that she move in with her when Stevie arrived in London.

'But I'll be in your way,' Stevie had demured.

'Nonsense,' Marissa had waved all Stevie's hesitations away with elder-sister authority. 'The flat's quite big enough and I'm off on assignments such a lot. Besides, I have to keep an eye on you, save you for only the very best of the big bad London wolves.'

Stevie had grimaced, but accepted. London flats were expensive and hard to come by. Besides, she and Marissa got on so well that it broke all codes of sisterly battling or rivalry. They both laughed about it and determined that it was due to the fact that seeing each other had always been part of a holiday treat, rather than an everyday habit.

'We're a frightfully strange family,' Marissa stated in her primmest English schoolgirl tones.

'You bet your life,' Stevie concurred in broadest American.

These parodies of their own very different accents always brought on an attack of giggles. So did the looks of surprise on people's faces when either of them introduced the other as 'my sister'. 'But you sound quite unlike one another,' the person would protest. Stevie and Marissa would exchange looks of complicity and explain that this didn't alter the fact that they were nonetheless sisters.

The mystery of their difference had its source in a complicated set of parental arrangements. When Stevie was eight and Marissa eleven, their mother, a Londoner by origin, had decided that she could no longer put up with life in the small New England university town where their American father had a post. He, on his side, couldn't see his way to abandoning the government-funded research he was engaged in at the university.

With a reasonableness the girls had retrospectively grown to admire, their parents had argued out a possible pattern of life. Their mother would return to London with Marissa, who wanted nothing more than to live in the excitement of a big city; while Stevie, who was a skiing addict, would stay with their father. Holidays would be spent together on either side of the ocean, and since, given their father's post, these were not only frequent but extensive, the family found itself together often enough. Christmases were usually spent in snowy New England and the long summers were divided between England and America. The sisters corresponded regularly, chatted to their overseas parents on the telephone weekly, and grew up with their distinct voices.

Stevie bounded up the three flights of stairs, turned her key in the lock and shouted, 'Marissa, I'm back!'

'So I can hear.' Marissa threw her exuberant sister a mocking look, took her specs off and uncoiled her long body from the sofa where she had been snuggling, newspaper in hand. 'What's all the excitement about? And the packages? Are we celebrating something?'

Stevie danced into the spacious room which served as kitchen, dining room and drawing room all in one and handed the take-away to her sister as if it were a large bouquet of flowers.

'We're celebrating my first client. And my first disaster!'

'She's being mysterious again,' Marissa wryly addressed an invisible third person. Then with a wide smile which lit up her thickly lashed grey eyes, she got up from the sofa and grabbed the take-away from Stevie. 'Right, little sister, five minutes to wash while I set the table, and then you can tell me all.'

Stevie scrubbed the layer of city grime off her face and hands, passed a brush through her thick honey-gold hair, and in a flash was at her sister's side. Marissa was just placing some mats on the round pine table which stood in one corner of the room. Stevie paused to look at her sister's calm, graceful gestures. Even barefoot, in old jeans and sweatshirt, Marissa was decorous, and Stevie was drawn to give her a hug.

Marissa smiled, reached for some plates, dished the

food out on them, making sure that Stevie had at least twice as much as she did, and sat down. 'I'm all ears, little sister. From the beginning, please.'

Between mouthfuls, Stevie recounted the day's events—the rude and rugged photographer, the Genghis Khan of Marlboro Country. ('I tell you, Marissa. I could almost see the wild mustangs galloping in the background'), her unintended modelling debut ('Wonderful,' Marissa interjected, 'but watch that curry!'), his assumption that she was a man, the way she had stormed out of the studio.

'Who is this madman?' Marissa finally asked. 'All we need is another loony in the fashion world.'

'James Reid,' Stevie answered. 'Have you heard of him?'

'James Reid,' Marissa pondered for a moment and then exclaimed, 'Not *the* James Reid? No it can't be. Unless . . .'

It was Stevie's turn to be all ears. 'Who is *the* James Reid?'

'Oh, Stevie, you must know, you with your boundless knowledge of all photographers.'

Stevie sifted through the many names and images she had stored in her mind over all these last years during which photography had been a passion. But she drew a blank. 'I don't know.'

'Well, perhaps his pictures never made their way to the States. But here . . . well, if it's the same man, which I somehow doubt, he worked for all the big nationals in turn—a news photographer, a war photographer, I should say. Won lots of prizes for photo-journalism. Wherever there were guns, guerrillas, civil wars, mad dictators, James Reid was there, in the midst of it, sending home the most gruelling of images. Then, perhaps three, or maybe it was four years ago, I stopped seeing his name around. He disappeared. Now that I think about it, I probably assumed that he'd had his head blown off. But we would have heard about that. Still, it can't be the same man. He wouldn't turn to fashion.'

Stevie took this in and shrugged. 'This James Reid would be old enough. And he's certainly not new to cameras.' A clear image of James Reid as he stood absorbed in his work, his unchallengeable authority, came back to her. She tossed it away. 'Oh well, Mr Brewster will have to reveal all tomorrow. The rat, he should have filled me in today!'

Marissa got up to make some coffee. 'If it is *the* James Reid, be careful, little sister. Rumour had it that he was quite a man with the ladies.'

'Have you ever known me to be a lady?' Stevie quipped.

Marissa laughed. 'An altogether uncommon event!' Then looking at her sister ruefully, she added, 'On the other hand, perhaps a ladykiller is just what you need to spice up life a bit.' She poured Stevie a cup of coffee and suddenly clasped her hands to her head with a melodramatic gesture, 'I almost forgot. Quick, the telly! My new commercial is meant to be on tonight.'

Stevie switched on the telly and stretched out on the plush cream carpet in front of it. She loved its thick comfort. It reminded her of the living room at home in New England, where she had sprawled on many a night doing her homework in front of the flickering light provided by the screen. But then she loved this flat altogether with its blend of creams and muted browns, broken only by the lush greens of the plants both women carefully tended.

The news was on and they listened to the closing headlines.

'It should come soon after this,' Marissa said, relaxing into the depths of the sofa.

And then all at once there was Marissa Carr—as Marissa was known professionally—on the screen, her dark hair coiled smoothly into a sophisticated knot, her grey eyes luminous in her finely-boned face, as she held a crystal wine glass out to be filled.

'Just wait until you see what happens to glamour girl me,' Marissa chuckled. Before the words were out Stevie saw the waiter pour the wine well over the rim of the glass and all over Marissa's silky black gown, while he stared lasciviously at her cleavage. A half-humorous, half sultry voice in the background announced, 'You can never have enough of a good thing.'

'There they go again,' Stevie muttered, 'using women's bodies to sell products.'

'Oh, Stevie, it's funny. Where's your sense of humour?' There was a pleading note in Marissa's voice.

'I know, I know. But it still makes me angry.'

'Well, what are you doing, then, representing fashion photographers?' Marissa challenged her.

'You're right. I've been asking myself the same question,' Stevie grumbled, 'but I haven't much choice at this point about whom I *can* represent. Give me a few years.' She glanced at her sister's face. 'I'm sorry, Marissa, I'm just a boring old New England puritan. It's a terrific ad—really.'

'You're forgiven, you boring old puritan. In any case, it brought in a lovely lot of money. And we're shooting another tomorrow, so it's off for my beauty sleep.'

'Probably time I had some too.' Stevie stood up and switched off the television.

The two girls brushed their teeth in unison and caught each other's reflection in the bathroom mirror. They were almost the same height, and beneath the contrasting heads of honey-gold and lustrous reddy-black, their faces were not unlike: Marissa's slightly more fragile, slightly paler than Stevie's, but similar in bone structure. 'What a pair we make!' Stevie laughed.

'Mm,' said Marissa, her mouth full of toothpaste. 'If you ever want to earn a little more money, just come and join me.'

'No, thank you ma'am,' Stevie demured. 'After today, I'll stay well clear of the space in front of the camera!'

They kissed each other goodnight and Stevie went off to her room. It was one of the two bedrooms the flat contained, small but cosy, with a window which looked out on to spacious gardens and tall trees. Stevie had decorated the walls with some of her favourite photographs: a soft-focus Cartier-Bresson, a portrait of her dad sitting in front of the fire which she herself had taken, the memorable Steichen photo of the Flat-iron Building in a New York shrouded by mist. Over the bed she had thrown a bright Mexican blanket—the single item she had carried with her for years, no matter where she had lived.

Picking up the novel she was reading, Stevie stretched out on the bed. But she couldn't concentrate on her book. Her mind kept running over the events of the day, all of which crystallised in the figure of a single person: Genghis Khan. Was he indeed *the* James Reid? she wondered as she fell asleep.

CHAPTER TWO

THE thing to do, Stevie coached herself as she walked up the two flights of stairs which led to the Donne and Brewster offices in the heart of Soho, is simply to pretend that everything went swimmingly; that James Reid and I are meeting again today, just to look at some prints.

'Hello, hon!' a funny high-pitched cockney voice called out before Stevie had had a chance to come fully through the office door. 'And how was this morning's journey from the heights of Hampstead?'

'Simply thrilling, Jan.' Stevie grimaced a hello to the company receptionist, and walked towards the office she shared with Anthony Howell.

He was already at his desk and he greeted her with a questioning look. 'Hello, stranger, we were looking for you yesterday. Thought you'd run off with a vagrant photographer!' He looked out at her from under a shaggy mass of blond hair, his warm brown eyes full of curiosity.

Stevie laughed, 'Well, you can stop hoping! I'm back.'

'And my day is complete. It was getting dreary in here yesterday, with nothing to look at but those rows and rows and rows of files.' Anthony punctuated his words with jerky head movements which followed the pattern of the photographic files lining two entire walls of their office.

'Well, now you can feast your eyes on me,' Stevie flashed him a provocative smile,' for all of five minutes, that is. Then I have to pay a visit to Mr Brewster.'

'Not before you've told me all about your meeting

with James Reid, photographer *extraordinaire*.'

'So *you* know about him,' Stevie threw him an accusing glance. 'Why didn't you brief me?'

'First of all, my young American miss, I didn't get much of a chance, did I. You rushed out of the office yesterday like Flash Gordon racing Superman —I shall have to call you Hurricane Stevie from now on. And secondly, I assumed that our venerable head had done the honours.' Anthony looked at her pityingly. 'Don't tell me you didn't know who he was!'

Stevie shook her head. 'Little innocent me launched into the fray by the Brewster! I had to wait until I got home in the evening to learn all about this James Reid from my sister. He is the war photographer, isn't he?' She looked at Anthony expectantly, not sure whether she wanted this first client of hers to be *the* James Reid or not.

Anthony shook his head and stretched to his full height, which was not inconsiderable, Stevie noted, when he bothered to stand straight. 'Such abysmal ignorance! Don't they teach you anything in these university photography courses?'

'Not much,' Stevie bantered back, 'or at least not much about this tiny island of yours. That's your job, Professor Howell.'

Stevie said it jokingly, but in fact it was from Anthony, whose assistant she had been hired to be, that she had learned almost everything she now knew about practising British photographers and the mechanics of agenting. She was grateful to him, for though he occasionally poked fun at her ignorance, he was always ready to help and cover up for any blunders she made. Over the past months, Stevie had learned some of the ropes: how to provide publishers, writers, magazine editors, T.V. researchers with specific existing prints that they wanted, or supply an array of photographic material for various projects which needed illustration.

She knew the kind of work most of the agency photographers could do and had met many of them personally. But the previous day's meeting with James Reid marked the first time she had personally been asked to handle a new account.

Turning serious, Anthony now rapidly filled her in on Reid's background. With a little more precision than her sister, he went over what was fundamentally the same material. 'What none of us knows,' he added, 'is why Reid gave it all up, what he's been doing these last years, and why he's suddenly turned up wanting to do fashion. It's hardly his line. Did you discover anything, Stevie?'

Stevie shrugged and shook her head. 'I didn't even get to first base. No one warned me about what I was getting into. But today will be different,' she added defiantly. 'I'm meeting him this afternoon.'

'Well, I can't think of anyone better placed to get Reid's trust. Just bat your lashes at him innocently and ...'

'Watch those sexist innuendos, Mr Howell, or I'll report you to the local sex discrimination officer,' Stevie threatened, and then taking in Anthony's dismayed expression, she burst out laughing. 'What I really want to know is why I've been assigned to handle James Reid. He seems a little too important for little unimportant me.'

It was Anthony's turn to laugh. 'Probably for those very reasons your sex discrimination officer would scowl at. Don't get huffy, Stevie, but I imagine that our most excellent boss took one whiff of Reid, remembered his reputation of being hard to handle, assessed the power of your green eyes,' Anthony skimmed the length of Stevie's body reflectively, 'and a little light went on in his head. You should be pleased, Stevie. If Reid is as good at fashion as he was at everything else, this could make your name in the agenting world.'

'Or ruin me for ever,' Stevie groaned, remembering

how little impression of any kind she had made on James Reid.

Anthony patted her shoulder comfortingly. 'Let's see if one of the collections in the library has some of Reid's past work in it. We've never dealt with him, so there won't be a personal file.'

Stevie followed Anthony to the large room which served as a reference library. Here the walls were given over to bookshelves rather than files. Anthony browsed for a moment. 'Yes, here we are.' He took a heavy handsome volume off one of the shelves, flicked through it and placed it on the small reading table. Reversed out on a black page, Stevie read, *The Middle East*. Under the title there were three photographers' names and among them, James Reid. She turned the pages of the book and looked closely at Reid's photographs.

'They're good, very good,' she breathed. The photographs here were mostly of refugee camps and prisoners of war. With a total lack of sensationalism, they made a statement about the suffering and injustice. Their harsh contrasts had a simplicity which suggested a life beyond the moment in which the individual photographs were taken, so that rather than looking at a news 'event', radically set apart from any continuity of life, Stevie felt as she turned the pages that individual histories were unfolding beneath her eyes. As she compared these photographs mentally with so many of the news pics she had seen, she felt almost in awe of James Reid's talent. These photographs suggested a man quite different from the rude, almost surly character she had met yesterday.

She voiced her feelings to Anthony.

'Yes, he's a rather special talent. I can't make out why he's given all this up.' Anthony and Stevie looked at each other in secret complicity and laughed. They both shared a contempt for fashion photography which they didn't dare voice to anyone else in the office, especially since it was generally acknowledged that Stevie was designated to build up that department.

Just a few weeks before Stevie had applied to the agency for the post they had advertised, the woman who had launched Donne and Brewster into fashion work—which for an agency of this kind was a new area, an American import—had left to set up her own firm. She had taken with her the agency's small but reputable list of fashion photographers. Fashion had turned out to be a potentially lucrative side of the business, and in his own cautious way, Mr Brewster wanted to see it built up again.

Stevie knew that she had been hired not on her personal merits alone. Yes, it was true that she had studied photography, had even spent one summer working in a New York photo library, and another as an apprentice to a local newspaper photographer. But she also knew that her mother's position as an editor of one of London's main women's magazines, plus the fact that her sister, Marissa Carr, was a top model, had helped not a little. She couldn't altogether blame Mr Brewster. When it came down to it, the fashion world was not so very large, and contacts helped. Stevie's lunchtime meetings with various fashion magazine editors—arranged not only to get to know them, but also to sniff out what might be the coming trends—owed some of their success to the fact that she was Susannah Henderson's daughter. And the dinners at her mother's house where she again bumped into the people she had to deal with professionally played their part as well. Having met her socially over dinner, these same people politely and promptly returned her calls, and made time to see her if she asked for it. So all in all, Stevie reflected, Mr Brewster had made a wise choice in hiring her—or so she hoped.

She went in to see him now, praying he wouldn't pry too deeply into her meeting with James Reid.

'Mr Brewster?' Stevie knocked at the door which was slightly ajar.

'Come in, Stevie,' Mr Brewster's voice boomed through the door. 'I've been waiting to see you.'

Stevie walked in and stood in front of Mr Brewster's glass and chrome desk. His was the only office in the firm which contained design furniture: strangely shaped lamps, outlandish filing systems, the newest and best from high tech designers. It always reminded Stevie of a visit to an office equipment exhibition. In this context, Mr Brewster looked quite out of place. He was a big, burly man who always wore impeccable but countrified tweeds and whom one imagined sitting by a blazing fireside, while he stroked an equally big and burly dog and smoked an after-dinner pipe.

He now looked Stevie up and down with an unconsciously appreciative nod and motioned her towards a chair.

'Well, young lady, how did it go yesterday? Have we got ourselves an outstanding new fashion photographer?'

Stevie took a deep breath. 'We'll know later on this afternoon. I'm meeting Mr Reid again then.'

'Wonderful, Stevie. That's simply wonderful!' Mr Brewster was all congratulations. 'I knew if anyone could cajole him into a good temper, you could.'

Stevie flushed, realising the enormity of her lie. But Mr Brewster simply assumed it was the result of his praise. 'I didn't dare tell you yesterday, but James Reid already had a run in with his own agency, when they wouldn't handle fashion work; and Leila—you know, the woman who used to work here and set up her own firm—well, she had one meeting with James Reid and sent him packing . . . in our direction, I'm happy to say. She rang to warn me and told me he needed someone patient and dedicated to deal with all his demands. So I immediately thought of you.'

Mr Brewster smiled at Stevie paternally. 'I'm very grateful.' She didn't know whether she had quite managed to keep the edge of sarcasm out of her voice.

Brewster *would* try her on someone no one else would touch!

'Is he as difficult as they all say?' Mr Brewster was angling for a little descriptive gossip.

Stevie wouldn't satisfy him. 'He's not the politest man I've ever met,' was all she offered him—and then added, 'but quite brilliant.'

'Good, good. Mr Brewster was almost rubbing his hands. 'Bring some prints back with you. I'm curious to see what he does with fashion.'

No more than I am, Stevie thought to herself, remembering James Reid's studio with its strange geometric shapes.

She went back to her office, sifted through the morning's post and began the daily round of fulfilling requests. Much of this was run-of-the-mill work and though Stevie usually did it with enthusiasm, today she found herself looking at her watch every half hour. Time was dragging. She sent off a set of prints by a French photographer, whose work some magazine had asked for; began to sift through her list of cookery photographers, so that she could submit some sample prints to a publisher who was planning a new series of European cookery. Then she typed out some permissions letters. But on the dot of four, she jumped up from her desk, like some Jack-in-the-box who had been coiled for too long, and announced to Anthony, 'I'm off.'

'Good luck, Stevie,' Anthony threw her a mocking wink. 'Don't let the great man do you down.'

'No danger of that,' Stevie exclaimed, pretending a courage she didn't altogether feel.

She picked up her large canvas bag and made for the cloakroom. A glance in the mirror showed flushed cheeks and hair in disarray. Stevie splashed some cold water over her face and brushed some order into her thick mane. 'You're just like some adolescent preparing for a first date,' she mocked herself, thinking of how that morning she had dressed very carefully and then deliberately changed into old clothes, so that James Reid wouldn't assume he had impressed her in any way.

Stevie waved a hurried goodbye to Jan at reception and ran down the stairs. The streets were already jammed with rush hour traffic, so she opted for the tube, not her preferred means of transportation since it meant she missed out on London sights. But she couldn't afford to be late today. James Reid might just assume she wasn't taking him up on his offer of an appointment and go off somewhere.

She arrived at his Chelsea mews with ten minutes to spare and passed the time by wandering round the streets, wondering how best to handle him and any brusqueness she might encounter. On the stroke of five, she rang the large brass bell.

The person who opened the door was not James Reid, but a young man of about twenty-five wearing snugly fitting jeans and a white Indian cotton shirt. Stevie stilled her dismay: was James Reid not going to be there after all? She announced herself as coolly as she could.

'I'm Stevie Henderson from Donne and Brewster. Mr Reid is expecting me, I believe.'

The young man flashed her a brilliant smile, 'I'm Claude, James's assistant. He'll be through in a few minutes.'

Claude ushered her into a room just opposite the changing room she remembered so well, offered her a cup of coffee and then excused himself. He had to help put the day's garments away and then hurry off to the darkroom. As he left, he gestured towards a pile of magazines and flashed her another brilliant smile.

Stevie tried to relax into the wide leather armchair. Her eyes flicked over the objects in the room. Though it obviously served as James Reid's office, it was an impersonal sort of place: a mahoganny desk, devoid of clutter; an old-fashioned glass-fronted bookcase which seemed from a cursory glance to be full of historical and political books. There were no photographs on the walls; the only ornament was a large blue and white vase which stood on a windowside table. Stevie leafed through one of the magazines which lay on an old wooden chest by her side.

It was a French fashion magazine. She chuckled. James Reid had been doing his fashion homework. A familiar face caught her eye and she paused to look at it carefully. Of course, it was Irena, the blonde model she had met here yesterday. Stevie checked the title of the magazine and whistled through her teeth. Irena couldn't come cheap. James Reid was certainly pulling out all the stops! If Irena had the kind of reputation which made her a feature in this magazine, then Stevie would have no trouble placing James Reid's work—unless his photographs were completely amateurish.

She looked through another publication in a strange language—Swedish, she determined at last—and caught her breath. Here again was Irena and this time the photographer's name was clearly marked as James Reid. So he wasn't altogether new to this world, Stevie thought.

She suddenly felt she needed to look her best for him, and on an impulse, she made her way to the remembered changing room. As she opened the door, she saw James Reid's assistant, patting a tearful woman on the shoulder. The woman looked up, startled, and when she took in Stevie, gave her a poisonous glance.

'I'm sorry,' Stevie mumbled, recognising the blonde model, Irena Borg. 'I was just looking for the loo.'

Above Irena's bent head, Claude gestured Stevie smilingly towards a door. She closed it behind her with relief and immediately turned the tap on so as not to overhear their voices. But despite that, Irena's sobs were clear.

'He just doesn't make any time for me any more,' Stevie heard her say. And then Claude's calming,

'There, there—he's nervy, that's all; he's working too hard.'

Stevie quickly dabbed some blusher on her cheeks, brushed her hair and made to flee. She didn't want to hear any of this. Reid seemed quite enough of a formidable brute without her learning sordid details about his private life.

She nodded briefly to Claude, again murmured apologies and raced back to the relative safety of the study. But no sooner had she lowered herself into the comfort of the armchair, than she was aware of a presence behind her. Stevie jumped to her feet, almost colliding as she turned with James Reid himself. He stretched out a large hand and she took it, feeling the strength of the man behind the slight pressure of his touch.

'Good afternoon, Ms Henderson. I'm so glad you decided to venture back here.' Stevie detected a sardonic gleam in his eyes, an unnecessary emphasis on the word Ms, but his voice was polite enough.

He gestured her back towards her chair, poured himself a cup of coffee from the pot, which seemed to have a ready supply, and eased his rugged body into a chair facing hers. Stevie found herself noting that for such a big man, he moved with remarkable grace. But the room suddenly grew too small to contain him, airless. With his rough checked shirt and well-worn jeans, he looked as if he belonged out of doors, in open spaces, where the coiled energy she sensed in him would find a ready release. She chased these meaningless thoughts from her head and concentrated on being professional.

James Reid picked up the magazine she had been looking at.

'So you've been examining Irena,' his chuckle made Stevie uncomfortable. 'She's not bad—moves well, takes instruction.'

Stevie took care not to be riled by the patronising

note in his voice. Instead she focussed on something she had failed to notice before—a slight accent. Of course, he was Scots. The burr didn't always show, but it was there, giving certain words a particular emphasis, a rugged music to his phrases.

'Have you lost your voice, Ms Henderson? Did I frighten you so badly yesterday?' Stevie realised she had said almost nothing since he had come into the room. He was distinctly laughing at her, though his tone was still polite.

'Not at all, Mr Reid,' she rose to the challenge. 'I just thought you were unspeakably rude, not to say arrogant.'

This time he laughed outright, a deep jagged sound from the depths of his chest. Stevie felt the colour rising to her cheeks.

'And I rightly said you were combative.' His laughter stopped abruptly. 'Shall we get down to business, Ms Henderson?' His tone all at once was distinctly menacing.

'That's what I'm here for,' Stevie met him on it.

'Good, good.' He cleared his throat. 'As you know, I haven't done any fashion photography until recently,' he pointed to the Scandinavian magazine, 'and none here. But I am one of the best photographers in Britain. I've come to you rather than going straight to the mags, because I can't be bothered with all the leg work. It's worth the percentage.' He looked at her critically, before continuing. 'I expect to work on my terms. I want my first three fashion features to go only into the best magazines; after that, when the commissions start rolling in, I don't want to be told which models to use, where to photograph them, or how . . .'

Stevie broke in. 'Aren't you asking a little too much before even having shown me some samples of your work, let alone placed any of it here?' No wonder the other agencies had sent this man packing. He was insufferable!

He rose and looked down on her from his looming height with icy blue-grey eyes. 'Ms Henderson,' his voice dripped contempt, 'I think I'm probably a better judge of my work and its worth than you are, let alone any of your fashion editors. And if your agency can't take me on trust and work for me wholeheartedly, rather than pandering to the buyers' flimsy taste, then we'd better part company now.' With three long strides he was at the door and poised to open it.

Stevie's anger found vent in her words. 'Mr Reid, I happen to know that you've already crossed swords with two of the better agencies. If you don't mind the hassle of handling your own work, then that's fine. Otherwise . . .' she let her voice trail off and was ready to leave by the door Reid hadn't yet quite opened when she heard a knock and a soft voice calling, 'James!'

'Sit down, Ms Henderson.' James Reid's tone carried an incontrovertible order and Stevie, who suddenly had an image of herself reporting to Mr Brewster on the outcome of this meeting, obeyed with unusual alacrity.

The door opened on to Irena's willowy form. The model took in Stevie's presence, nodded, and then focussed her large blue eyes on James Reid. 'Where shall I meet you tonight, James?' Stevie overheard her soft, accented voice.

'Not tonight, Irena, I've too much work to do.' He passed a large hand through his dark curly hair and to counterpoise the brusqueness of his tone, offered the girl some coffee.

She accepted it gratefully, but since he didn't ask her to sit down, she drank it quickly and gave him a fleeting kiss. With an unsteady smile, she said, 'I'll see you tomorrow, then.'

James Reid squeezed her shoulder and nodded. Then he turned to Stevie, who looked upon the scene disapprovingly.

'Have you had a chance to reconsider, Ms

Henderson?' His tone was polite again, but he looked tired.

'Mr Reid,' Stevie measured her words, 'of course Donne and Brewster would like to represent you; but we can't work miracles, make promises that we couldn't possibly keep.'

He let out a long breath. 'Yes, yes, of course,' he pushed her words aside. 'What I want to find out is if you'll commit yourself to trying?' He held her eyes for a moment.

Stevie shrugged. 'I'll do my best. That goes without saying. But Mr Reid, if you won't show me what you can do, it's rather difficult for me to commit myself to your work wholeheartedly, let alone sell it. Your name alone is no guarantee of anything, no matter how illustrious it may be.'

His face was suddenly warm with laughter. 'I can see I've found myself a real taskmaster,' he said. 'Yes, Ms Henderson, I'll show you evidence, give you proof of what I can do.' He walked out of the room still laughing, leaving Stevie feeling like a schoolgirl who had just been outwitted.

But she hadn't been, she assured herself as she waited for his return. After all, Mr Brewster did want her to come back with this prize client, even if it meant—her heart sank as she contemplated the difficulty—she would then be responsible for placing his work and getting him more. Not an easy thing in this highly competitive world. She would have to take the measure of James Reid, woo him into slightly more compliant behaviour. Time to bring out the charm, young lady, she said to herself. There are ways of making men amenable.

She rose from her chair, smoothed her trousers, adjusted her jacket belt and ran her fingers through her hair, pushing it away from her face so that its fine lines were evident.

Soundlessly James Reid was next to her, and out of

sheer surprise Stevie swallowed hard. She hoped he hadn't caught her preening herself, but one look at him told her he was quite oblivious to her appearance, and intent only on the prints he carried. Charming him was not going to be a simple matter.

While he was laying some photographs out on the desk, she watched him out of the corner of her eye. There was a brooding intensity in the jagged planes of his face, a strength to the square jaw which suggested determination. The lips were strangely full, yet the lines around them spoke of a singleness of purpose rather than sensuality. Stevie smiled to herself: yes, he was what her mother, taking on her look of wry wisdom, would have called a man. The word on her lips always spoke sentences.

'Do you think you might look at these prints now that I've bothered to get them, Ms Henderson?' James Reid asked sardonically.

Stevie frowned and then, remembering her resolution, put on her most charming smile, 'Do call me, Stevie, Mr Reid. Ms Henderson makes me feel decidedly uncomfortable.'

'Yes, yes,' he flicked her comment aside like some meaningless bit of conversational fluff.

Stevie focussed her attention on the prints and let out an audible gasp. 'But these are all of me!'

'What difference does it make whom they're of? They're photographs, aren't they? You're wearing clothes, aren't you?'

Stevie could find no answer to that which fell into the category of being charming, so she tried to concentrate critically on the prints. There was an odd quality to them, a starkness, which made woman, background, garments, quite distinctly separate. She rather liked the total lack of glamour. But that was precisely why they wouldn't do. She decided to say nothing, and motioned for him to show her some more.

He looked at her steadily. 'Don't bother telling me.

They're not for your mags, I know that. But I thought you might like them—in case you decide to work in front of the camera at some point.' He handed her the bundle of photographs.

Stevie looked at him in astonishment. 'Not me!' she stated emphatically. 'But thank you, I'd like to have them, as a memento of my one and only modelling achievement.'

Suddenly he smiled at her warmly and the light played in his blue eyes. 'Good, good,' he muttered. 'Now look at these.'

He laid out a sequence of Irena wearing frothy lace and ambling along the seashore. Her cloud of white-gold hair blew across the misty soft focus of her face, so that she looked like a figure out of an old sepia print. He was scrutinising her response and Stevie, swallowing a little lump of envy as she thought of how badly the pictures of her compared with the evident glamour of Irena, just managed to meet his eyes and say, 'These are perfect.'

His look was contemptuous. 'Yes, I know they are. They fall right into the mould, don't they? Just right for your fashion editors. All that ephemeral glamour totally unrelated to life is just what they want.' His eyes scanned the photographs derisively.

'If that's how you feel about it, why on earth are you doing fashion photography!' Stevie brought it out with a scolding emphasis.

He examined her coldly for a moment, then let out a mirthless chuckle. 'Someone dared me. Said I could only photograph misery—a skilled habitual tick. So I'm proving to the world that that isn't the case. Does that satisfy you?'

Stevie searched his face. Its grimness somehow belied his explanation, but she let it pass. She didn't want to risk alienating him again and she turned her attention to the sequences he was now laying out before her: Irena in bright disco-coloured minis leaning jauntily against a video juke-box; Irena in a white overall fiercely clinging to the bars of a motorbike; and so it went on with a variety of models until Stevie felt quite dazed.

'Have you had your proof yet?' His voice was mocking.

'Ample proof,' Stevie replied, and trying to make up for her earlier bluntness, she added, 'These prints are wonderful. And your models, especially Irena, are beautiful.' Her tone was a little wistful.

'Beautiful perhaps,' his voice held an unnecessary hardness, 'but a greater lot of narcissistic wretches the world has never seen.' He flung Stevie a scathing glance which implicated her in his remarks. 'The world would be a better place without them. If I ever settle down—which is highly unlikely—give me a good plain Jane with a modicum of intelligence who cares for more than her body.'

Stevie bristled, 'It's hardly the models' fault. It's you men who want the women to look like that. You who . . .'

'Read the fashion magazines?' Reid scoffed. 'Don't give me that nonsense.'

He was hateful, Stevie thought, her eyes burning into his. Hateful! He had made her lose her thread and he was mocking her openly. A passing thought of Marissa fuelled her anger and made the words tumble out of her. 'Be that as it may, Mr James Reid, right now you're dealing with the fashion world and your plain Janes, good as they may be, aren't going to sell you any photographs. Neither are they going to sell any clothes, which is what they're there for in the first place.'

'Touché,' he laughed. 'On that score we almost agree, if you'll kindly remember these prints,' he gestured at the desk. 'And what we need is for you to get me three or four top commissions on the strength of these. I'll follow instructions to a T. Then I want a free hand to do as I please.' It was uttered almost as a threat.

Stevie wondered what he might do when he had, as he said, a free hand. But for the moment, she replied simply, 'I'll do my best.'

Let's hope it's good enough Ms Henderson,' he muttered.

Stevie was about to lash out at him again, but she remembered just in time how important it was for her to charm him. She suddenly had an inspiration. 'Well, now that that's settled, why not let me take you out to dinner to seal our agreement?'

His eyes turned a steely grey and he looked at her angrily. 'The trouble with working women is that the lines between business and pleasure get insupportably blurred.' His gaze flickered over her body and when it rested on her face again, his expression had changed. 'But why not indeed? American women are relatively tolerant in these matters, I believe, and are allowed a little forwardness.'

Stevie bridled, but met his challenge. 'Oh yes, Mr Reid, especially when they're entertaining important clients,' she said with mock sweetness.

'That's all right, then,' his eyes glinted irony. 'But we'll have to make it another evening—I'm tied up tonight. Let's say Tuesday. Perhaps by then you may have some news for me as well.'

'We can only hope, Mr Reid,' Stevie said as calmly as she could.

She bundled the prints into folders and made for the door. Just before she reached it, he called out, 'By the way, Ms Henderson, now that you're about to entertain me, do call me James. It will make the transition into pleasure a little easier.'

Stevie threw him a fiery glance. Hateful ogre! she thought to herself as she marched out of the house.

The following evening Stevie looked again and again through the few party dresses her cupboard held. Then, pausing for a moment, she pulled out a dress she had

already examined once: a black silk shantung, simply
cut in front, but with a plunging silver-laced vee at the
back and two provocative slits up the sides. Marissa
had picked it up at one of the couture house sales she
frequented and presented it to Stevie when she first
arrived in London.

'That's what you'll need for the parties you'll be
going to,' she had said, showing off the sophisticated
garment with all the enthusiasm of a connoisseur.

Stevie had swallowed her 'Never!' and offered the
most gracious thank you she could muster. But the
dress had stayed well to the back of her wardrobe,
unworn. 'I'm not in the mood,' she had said to Marissa
every time her sister had suggested she put it on.

Now she looked at the dress reflectively. It was
exactly what Mr Brewster's party called for. Dinner
jackets, he had stipulated to Anthony in Stevie's
hearing, and she knew what that meant where she was
concerned.

Reaching for a pair of sheer tights, she pulled them
up her shapely legs, put on a pair of elegant high-heeled
shoes, and then eased the dress over her shoulders. She
went to look at herself in Marissa's three-cornered
mirror. The dress moulded her shape suggestively, its
silken black providing a dramatic contrast to her tawny
skin and gleaming honey-gold hair.

Stevie's image thrust her into momentary confusion.
This wasn't her usual casual, exuberant self, but a
different woman with a hint of mystery in her green
eyes. With a puritan shudder, Stevie moved to take the
dress off, and then stopped herself. If she was attractive,
as she had been told often enough over the years, then
she might as well face up to it within herself. In any
case, she thought a little muddledly, it makes no
difference to me and it will please Mr Brewster.

The feel of the silk over her hips, the high heels, made
her move quite differently and with sudden impishness,
she applied just a little more make-up than usual to her

green eyes, bringing out their emerald depths beneath the gold-blonde of her hair. She rummaged in Marissa's closet and brought out a Spanish silk shawl, strewn with bold red flowers and green leaves. This, with the sense of a little girl masquerading, she flung lavishly over one shoulder. As she looked at herself critically, she decided on a final touch, some deeply red lipstick and a little more blusher on her cheeks.

No sooner had she finished dressing than the doorbell rang. Anthony's low whistle as he walked into the flat brought a flush to her face. He looked at her in exaggerated astonishment.

'Hurricane Stevie transforms herself into Stephanie, seductive temptress. Tune back later in the evening to see her do battle in the wilds of Hampshire.' His familiar comic book allusions made her laugh.

'Do I look dreadful, Anthony? Shall I change?'

'Only if you're afraid I won't be able to beat off the male hordes.' He threw his shoulders back and beat his chest, Tarzan fashion.

Stevie giggled. 'A high heel aimed in the right direction will do the trick adequately, I think.'

'Well then, we're off.' He opened the door for her with a low bow.

Stevie smiled, 'You're looking quite the dashing gentleman yourself, Anthony Howell, so stop making fun of me.' She took in the brushed fair hair above the smooth brow, the immaculately white dinner jacket and ruffled shirt Anthony wore.

'Your flattery is honey to my ears, Stevie darling.' He gave her his arm.

'Oh,' Stevie suddenly rushed into her own room and came running back, 'I almost forgot James Reid's prints. Feast your eyes on these for a minute, Anthony.'

Anthony examined the photographs carefully.

'Well?' Stevie prodded him a little.

'Well, they're fine,' he said at last, 'very skilled. As if he'd studied all the best photographers and thrown in

just a little, not too much, of himself. I don't
understand it.'

Stevie leapt to James Reid's defence. 'What do you
expect him to do? He has to break into the field, and
you don't start by revolutionising everything.'

Anthony looked at her curiously. 'You'll make a very
good agent, Stevie, but don't try to sell him to me. I'm
on your side, remember? I was just looking for the Reid
touch, the starkness, the humanity.'

Stevie burst into giggles. 'You sound just like him!
Both of you full of contempt for this,' she gestured at
the fashion prints.

'Well, why is he doing it, then?'

'I haven't the foggiest. I work for a photographic
agency, not a detective agency, as you know. But I'll
find out,' Stevie added as much to herself as to
Anthony.

They made their way to Hampshire companionably.
Anthony drove quickly through traffic-free streets and
then on to the motorway, while Stevie told him about
her meeting with James Reid, omitting as she was
painfully aware, the details which had most forcibly
struck her.

They arrived in the village where Mr Brewster lived
just as the spring sun was beginning to set, suffusing
wisteria-covered cottages in its pink glow and setting off
their grey local stone to perfection.

'This is delicious,' Stevie murmured. 'Nothing like it
in the U.S. of A.'

'It's what we English do best, don't you know, Stevie?
We have a genius for villages. And here we are, the
gentrified Brewster residence.' Anthony pulled the car
into a long tree-lined drive and stopped in front of a
rambling two-storey house, already resonant with sound.

'I didn't know the firm was quite so successful,' said
Stevie, looking round the well-tended grounds which
seemed to stretch into miles of fields.

Anthony chuckled, 'It's the family home. But I dare

say old Brewster doesn't do too badly either. Now mind you don't let yourself be tantalised away by one of the local lords, Stevie, 'cause they sure as Jeeves are going to make one helluva lunge at your democratic profile.' He threw Stevie an appraising look as she swung shapely legs out of the car and smoothed her dress over her hips. 'Ready?'

'Ready as I'll ever be,' Stevie nodded a little nervously.

Anthony rang the bell and the door was opened almost instantly by a man in impeccable evening dress who greeted them formally.

'The proverbial butler,' Anthony whispered.

'Not one of the local lords I have to beware of,' Stevie teased him.

'They'll be a lot less proper,' Anthony winked, just as Mr Brewster emerged from a large, many-windowed room into the marbled hall to welcome them. Stevie looked round and noted the highly polished wainscoting, an enormous fireplace, a buffet table laden with trays, and groups of people here and there all engrossed in talk and laughter. She suddenly felt awkward, frightened.

Mr Brewster's warm greeting did a little to dispel her nervousness. 'Stevie, you do the firm proud.' He shook her hand firmly, giving her a quick admiring look, and led them both through a pair of the room's tall french windows into a flower-filled garden towards a group of laughing faces.

Stevie thought she would never remember the strings of names, but in the general run of chatter, it seemed to matter not at all. A glass of sparkling white wine had magically appeared in her hand and as she sipped its cool wetness, she noticed a tall, elegant man with piercing dark eyes and sun-bleached hair gazing at her reflectively.

Within seconds he was at her side, 'And who, might I ask, is this charming new presence in our midst?' His eyes flickered over her at a leisurely pace.

With a quick look round to make sure of Anthony's whereabouts, Stevie explained that she worked for Mr Brewster.

'Yes, my elder brother always did have amazingly good taste,' the man's eyes continued to rove across her body. 'I'm Tom—Tom Brewster,' he stretched out a hand and when Stevie took it he gave hers a perceptible squeeze. 'I'm here on a visit from Latin America. But you—you're American?' he queried.

'Oh gosh,' Stevie laughed, 'and here I thought I'd left my accent behind in New England!'

'Just as I thought I'd left mine behind in Old England when I reached Brazil. But it trails one.' Tom Brewster looked at her with interest. 'Where in New England? I've spent some time there.'

Stevie named the small college town where she had grown up.

'You don't by any chance know a physicist by the name of Gerald Epstein?'

Stevie's eyes grew wide. 'He works in my father's department.'

Tom Brewster chuckled, 'The proverbial small world again! The population grows, but the same two thousand people keep bumping into each other here and there across the globe.'

'And what do you do, if that's not too direct a question to ask of someone at an English country party?' Stevie queried.

'I lost my unbounded sense of privacy years ago,' Tom Brewster smiled at her. 'Why don't we have a little stroll round the grounds and I'll tell you all about myself—and the gardens too. I know them well.'

He gave her his arm and after a momentary hesitation and with a quick wave to Anthony who was engrossed in conversation, Stevie took it. There was little point in coming to a party of this kind and then being wary of every invitation.

Tom Brewster proved a pleasant companion. He was full of lore about Brazil, the excesses of carnival time, as well as the micro-chip firm which he managed.

The scent of early blooming honeysuckle and wisteria perfumed the warm evening, the flower beds were magnificent, and as they turned down a path and Stevie saw an open field and a brown mare grazing, she found herself giggling.

Tom looked at her strangely.

'I was only reflecting about how lucky I was to be here. It's every American girl's dream of what England is really like.'

Tom joined in her laughter. 'With the perfect Englishman at your side.'

'Despite the fact that he's now Brazilian . . .'

'Only in his approach to the ladies.' Tom draped an arm loosely over her shoulder.

Stevie flinched, but not wanting to appear childish, she didn't draw away. They turned down one of the several paths bordered by thick shrubbery. Just a few yards in front of them, a couple were wrapped in embrace. At their approach, the man looked up, and Stevie caught her breath as a violent pang shot through her. James Reid: yes, of course, Mr Brewster would invite him; and the woman with him was unmistakably Irena.

CHAPTER THREE

STEVIE veered away from Tom Brewster's arm and stumbled back along the path. But the image of the embracing couple stayed stubbornly in front of her. It's persistence, accompanied by the butterfly hordes invading her stomach, made her wonder at her own emotion. Could she be jealous? The word suddenly planted itself in her mind. Of a man she had only met twice and wasn't even sure she liked. She swept the thought away with a grimace and tried to focus on Tom Brewster's words as he once again took hold of her arm.

'A friend of yours?' he queried.

She nodded nonchalantly, not trusting her voice.

'The best remedy for that kind of surprise is homeopathic.' He drew her to him and placed a feathery kiss on her lips.

Stevie pulled away. 'I think a drink would be better medicine,' she said as lightly as she could.

'Whatever the beautiful lady orders,' Tom offered gallantly. 'And perhaps some food as well?'

She nodded.

Strains of soft music wafted through the open french windows of the house into the evening air. Couples were sitting at tables placed here and there round the large patio. One or two were already dancing. As Tom stood back for Stevie to precede him through the door, Anthony hailed her.

'Ready for some dinner, Stevie?' he looked at her and her companion expectantly, as if waiting for Stevie to make a sign.

Stevie introduced the two men, eager to have them chat so that she could recompose herself. They both

44

urged her to taste the various *hors d'oeuvres* spread on the long table: small caviar canapés, *bouches de reine* heaped with shrimp and mushroom, platters of cunningly arranged crudités. Stevie piled her plate high and followed the men to an outdoor table, stopping for a few moments on the way to greet a few familiar faces.

It was growing dark now and brightly coloured Chinese lanterns had been lit. They cast a wavering light over tables, patio, and grounds enveloping everything in an aura of mystery, a dreaminess which invaded Stevie so that she listened to the men's talk and her own as if through a haze.

The sound of a deep voice jarred her from her reverie. Stevie looked up and felt a warm flush covering her neck. James Reid stood there, the hollows of his strong face oddly shadowed in the lantern light. Stevie had never seen him in formal dress before and he looked, she had to admit it to herself, dangerously attractive, his hair savagely dark against the silky whiteness of a shirt stretched tautly over his powerful torso, his shoulders even broader in the charcoal-black evening suit.

'May we join you?' he asked directly of Stevie. She noted Irena in the shadows at his side.

'Of course,' Stevie responded, slightly breathless, gesturing to the two unfilled chairs at their table. She realised that the others didn't know James and willing herself into vivaciousness, she introduced them, American style, as she blithely called it, giving name, profession and enthusiastic credentials, all with just a hint of self-irony.

Tom Brewster laughed, 'I shall have to take you to Brazil as my official hostess. You'll do wonders for rather stiff business gatherings!'

'You can't possibly steal Stevie from us. We need her right here,' James smiled down at Stevie, but his tone carried an emphasis which made her catch her breath. It also brought a hostile glance from Irena, who looked like the angel maiden of Victorian romance, in a dress fashioned of creamy tiers of old-fashioned lace. But the expression on her face, almost hidden in loose ringlets, had nothing little-girlish about it, Stevie found herself thinking cattily as she watched Irena place her hand possessively on James's arm.

'It's an honour to meet you,' Stevie heard Anthony saying to James. I've been a long-time admirer of your work.'

James looked at him wryly. 'Let's hope you continue so, despite my present vagaries.'

'I'm rather curious to know why you've taken up this fashion work,' Anthony said.

James Reid's face darkened. 'I have my reasons,' he replied, testily, 'but they're not really for public consumption. Why, Mr Howell? Do you find my present work quite as laughable as I do?' he arched his eyebrows sardonically.

Anthony was about to protest politely when Irena intervened.

'James is always putting himself down,' she said protectively. 'It is silly, don't you think, Mr Howell? His fashion photographs are beautiful.'

'Not half so beautiful as you are in the flesh.' Anthony's eyes, despite his interest in James, were all for Irena. He looked as if he had been confronted by a vision.

'Rat!' Stevie thought. 'So much for his denunciations of glamour!' And with a flirtatiousness quite novel to her, she passed a hand langourously through her hair and turned her gaze to Tom Brewster.

'That Brazilian idea sounds tantalising. What would an official hostess do?'

Tom Brewster laughed huskily, 'Well, Stevie,' he traced the outline of her smile with a light touch, 'a lot of just that.'

Stevie caught a dangerous sparkle in James Reid's

eye as she queried Tom further, but before he could expound on the duties of an official hostess at greater length, James interrupted.

'Stevie wouldn't suit, Mr Brewster—she's far too headstrong. One wrong word and she's off and running. She'd alienate half your associates. Isn't that so, Stevie?' He threw her an intimate glance.

'Oh, I don't know. With the right inducement, I could learn to be pleasant, I'm sure.' She let her eyes rest for a moment on Tom Brewster's face. And then, before she could be taken up on any of this, she rose. 'But right now, I'm more interested in investigating the wonders of the buffet!'

'I'll join you.' James stood up before Tom could offer his company.

'Hurry back, Stevie,' he called after her, 'and we can discuss inducements.'

As they walked towards the dining room, James questioned her, a tinge of anger in his voice. 'What's all this about going to Brazil? Have you gone mad?'

'Oh, just checking out the scene,' Stevie drawled. Her head felt oddly light, as if she were floating.

'And all those things you implied about being committed to your work?' he asked sarcastically.

'Afraid to lose your agent?' She raised her eyes to his, their green depths flashing wickedly.

'As a matter of fact, I am.' He roughly took hold of her arm and steered her round some dancing couples and away from the dining room door towards one of the many paths which led through the grounds. 'Does that surprise you?' He stopped and looked deeply into her eyes, his own darkening with anger.

'Well, you're hardly my keeper, Mr James Reid. Just a client,' Stevie stated bluntly, realising all at the same time that she was treading in dangerous waters, that she was slightly drunk with wine and nervousness. She struggled away from his grip and continued down the path until it gave way to a small open space graced by a copper beech, its rust-coloured leaves dancing in the moonlight.

He caught up with her and forced her to face him. His eyes grazed over her face and lazily played over the length of her body moulded by the black silk dress. 'The word client has a strange ring to it, dressed as you are tonight,' he said sardonically.

Stevie's eyes opened wide in shock, but before she could find an answer, his arms were round her, pinioning her to him and his full lips were on hers, assaulting her senses with a ferocity she had never experienced before. Her blood seemed to be coursing wildly through her veins, setting up a throbbing in her ears, driving her arms round his shoulders to explore their muscular firmness, when she would rather have pummelled him hard. As his kiss became more searching, more mellow, she grew painfully aware of the caress of his hands through her thick hair, over her almost bare back, of the hardness of his thighs moulded against hers, and heat flooded through her. It seemed to light up a danger signal in her head, and despite the sensation that her legs would give way, she pushed him away from her.

There was a flicker of amusement in James's eyes as he met her shocked expression. It made Stevie's temper flare once more. 'I'm not one of your models, you know!' she lashed out at him, as an image of the embrace she had caught him in with Irena shook her.

'Oh, but you could so very easily be,' he taunted her, his gaze undressing her with a leisurely slowness.

'Not on your life, Genghis Khan, you're not my type!' Stevie was furious. But even through her anger, she recognised the lie of her words. No man had ever kindled her senses in this way, set up a tense trembling in her by his very proximity.

'You're very sure of that?' he surveyed her arrogantly, and uttered a low velvety laugh like a caress.

'Absolutely!' Stevie brought it out with a finality, though her limbs were shaking.

'Shall we put it to the test?'

Stevie drew away, turning her back on him and beginning to make her way back towards the others.

'And I imagine that blond charmer is your type?' his voice pursued her with a dangerous challenge.

'Perhaps he is.' Stevie's mouth again preceded her thoughts.

'Well, we'd better hurry back to him, hadn't we?' He gripped her arm fiercely and manoeuvred her towards the dining room.

Stevie tried to look at ease as the brighter light fell on them, but she felt shaky, as if she actually needed James's support. The realisation of that doubled her anger.

'I don't know why you're doing this,' she suddenly threw out at him, turning to confront him and pulling her arm away from his grip. 'You've made it quite clear that you have complete contempt for attractive women.'

'Have I now?' He looked at her sardonically and his look inflamed her further.

'Yes, contempt—except for a little exploitative escapade here and there,' Stevie pressed on, despite the fact that his eyes had narrowed dangerously. 'And by all reports, that's what I'm supposed to be—an attractive woman. And I'm not interested in either your contempt or your exploits!'

'Indeed?' He suddenly burst into laughter. With glinting eyes which seemed to scorch her skin, he conducted a slow, almost tactile examination of her face, her body, her legs. 'Not bad,' he said at last. 'Not perfect, but not bad. A little rounder than my starved models . . . I confirm the reports. But don't let it go to your head.'

Stevie's cheeks blazed at his open assessment. 'Nothing goes to my head, Mr Reid,' her voice was hot with anger. 'It's wonderfully, blissfully empty, as you've suggested it must be.'

She turned away from him and began to walk towards the house.

But he was right behind her. 'You know, Stevie,' his voice was suddenly charged, husky, 'the mind may dictate one thing and the eyes, the senses, register something quite different. Has it never happened to you?'

Stevie was saved the need to answer as Mr Brewster came up to them to make sure they were enjoying themselves. He engaged James in conversation, emphasising what Stevie was sure he had already said, how happy he was to have James with the firm. Excusing herself, Stevie slipped quietly away, remembering just in time to fill a plate before she rejoined the others.

In answer to Anthony and Tom Brewster's quizzical looks, she explained that she and James had been delayed by various acquaintances. 'He's still chatting to my boss, your brother,' she added to Tom, but for Irena's benefit. The woman had thrown her a scathing glance. Quite right, too, Stevie thought. If my man went off with someone else, I'd be in a right rage! Then with a sense of utter exhaustion, she sank gratefully into the chair Tom pulled out for her and toyed with the food on her plate. Her appetite had completely disappeared, as had her interest in what was being said. When Tom Brewster offered to fetch some more wine she acquiesced readily. Anthony was so deeply engrossed in Irena, it was almost as if she were alone, and that was, Stevie realised, what she wanted most: a solitary moment in which to reflect on the implications of James's last words, the change in his voice. But after far too short a time Irena slipped off, announcing that she wanted to freshen up a little, and Anthony turned to engage Stevie.

'She's wonderful,' he all but sighed into Stevie's ear. 'What a woman!'

Stevie quelled an impulse to laugh hysterically. 'And here I remember—was it just yesterday—you expressed yourself on the subject of glamour with something akin to derision.'

'Oh, but Stevie,' Anthony's brown eyes were wide, 'Irena's special.' He suddenly chuckled. 'I do believe I'm smitten!' He clutched his hands to his heart with an exaggerated gesture.

'Why don't you ask her to dance?' Stevie suggested as she saw Irena floating back to their table.

'Do you mind being left?' he asked.

'Go on!' She all but pushed him off, but before she had a chance to return to her thoughts, Tom was back and following the example of the other two, beckoned her to dance. Stevie acquiesced. It would be easier than having to talk. Then too, dancing was an activity she enjoyed and had missed since her university days when dancing parties were frequent. And though she was no expert, Tom Brewster guided her smoothly across the patio so that after a moment she forgot her fatigue and gave herself to the rhythmic movements.

It was with a start that she heard a low voice at her side intone, 'May I?'

She looked up to see James Reid in front of her and without pausing to think, she nodded.

His arms encircled her, his fingers resting gently and then more firmly on the bare stretch of her back. A tremor passed through her and she stiffened. 'Relax, little one,' he whispered through the mass of her hair. His breath warm on her ear set her pulses tingling, and noticing her response, he held her more closely to him.

With a last mute prayer to the gods of sanity, Stevie melted to the caressing pressure of his fingertips on her spine, allowing his taut form to mould hers, breathing in deeply the fresh, clean smell of his hair, his maleness. She stifled a gasp as his hands slipped down her hips, bringing her even more closely to him. She could feel the tight muscles of his thighs bending smoothly to the slow rhythms, the firm, fluid movements of his body which sent a warm tide through her, enveloping her in wave after luxuriant wave of sensation.

He held her to him even after the music had stopped, but as Stevie opened her eyes, she had the distinct sense that she was engaged in a midsummer madness. Everything about her, from the thumping of her heart to the odd heaviness in her limbs, was strange, unfamiliar. 'I think I'd better get home,' she said, her voice tremulous, lacking conviction, as if it came from an unknown distance.

'Your eyes are like two emerald pools, vast in a dream landscape,' James said huskily.

She pulled away, more insistent now and looked round for Anthony. 'I think I've had too much to drink,' she mumbled. 'I want to go.'

'I'll take you home,' he said, his arm still around her and his voice more a command than an offer.

'But I came with Anthony,' Stevie protested.

'Anthony seems very happily engaged.' James guided her eyes towards a dancing couple who seemed oblivious to their surroundings, and then ushering her towards a chair, went off in their direction. He was back almost as soon as he had gone. 'That's all arranged,' he said. 'Let's be off.'

Stevie looked at the man in front of her and was overcome by an impending sense of helplessness. He reached for her arm and pulled her out of the chair.

'And Irena?' Stevie tried to formulate a thought.

'Irena be damned,' James's voice was gruff. 'A new adoring man at her feet will do her a world of good.'

Stevie allowed herself to be led puppet-like through the crowded house, managed to exchange a few words and politely thank their host and hostess. Just as they were about to leave, Tom Brewster caught up with her. 'I'll be in touch, Stevie,' he said, avoiding Reid, and holding her hand firmly for a moment in his.

And then they were out in the murmuring quiet of

the country night. 'Coxcomb!' Stevie thought she heard James grumble before he placed an arm possessively round her shoulders. His car was parked a little way up the tree-lined drive and they walked silently side by side.

As they approached the white Jaguar, James impatiently pulled off his bow tie. Letting out a deep breath, he turned her round to face him. In the moonlight his features seemed chiselled out of stone and as he grazed the curve of her cheek with his fingers, Stevie found herself raising her lips to his. They met in a long probing kiss which seemed to invade her entire body. She arched beneath his insistent touch and a small moan escaped her as he folded her in an embrace that set all her senses aflame. With a gesture quite new to her, Stevie fingered his taut chest, the rough texture of hair beneath the smooth column of his neck. Suddenly consumed by the desire to feel his skin against her bare flesh, her hand reached beneath the silk of his shirt to flow over the satin of his shoulders.

Gently James stopped her. His eyes, black in the moonlight, glinted, posed a question. 'Shall I take you home with me, Stevie?' he asked, his voice gruff as he motioned her towards the car door.

Stevie slid on to the leather seat, her heart setting up a beating she was sure could be heard as far as the Brewster house. What are you doing, Stevie Henderson? she asked herself beyond its mad thudding. This man isn't a little boy to be played with. If you continue as you are doing, you have no right to come out of this evening unscathed. And you barely know this man. And you have to work with him. And yes, you desire him. She was suddenly overwhelmed by the accuracy of the word. Desire—it was not something she had ever experienced before. But where would it lead?

As James lowered his lithe form into the seat next to hers, she met his eyes. His arm reached out to embrace her, his lips claimed her, this time travelling down her

neck then the hollow between her breasts with their heat.
Her body responded to his touch with a passion that
startled her. Her heart set up a wild tattoo. Before its
beating could engulf her totally, she drew away,
conjuring up a hovering image which worried the very
edge of her mind: Jordan. Jordan Richards, the one
constant man in her life. How could this stranger have
eradicated him so thoroughly from her thoughts by the
sheer magnetism of his presence? Stevie searched
desperately for a voice which could drown the beating
of her pulse. It emerged as a comic American drawl
which almost masked the measure of her mounting
nervousness.

'You're too fast for me, Mr James Reid—much too
fast! I'm just a simple small-town girl, and there's this
man I know back home, who counts on me, trusts me.'

James looked at her with disbelief for a long moment.
His face seemed to turn white with repressed fury. With
an angry gesture he started the engine, pushed the car
into gear, making it lunge forward with a savage roar.

'Oh dear,' Stevie muttered out loud, trying to be
funny, 'I've said the wrong thing again!'

In the darkness, she could sense rather than see the
blazing look he threw at her. A fleeting light showed
tensed fingers gripping the steering wheel, a stern
impenetrable profile. She wanted desperately to touch
him, but she kept her hands clenched at her side.

Jordan's image haunted her. How could she have
come so close to betraying him, when only a week ago
she had written to him and intimated that, exciting
as her work and London might be, there were certainly
no new men in her life. And now . . .

She stole a covert glance at James and then screwed
her eyes tightly shut to obliterate his presence. The cool
strains of Miles Davis filled the car and she let them lull
her away across the Atlantic to the small town where
she and Jordan Richards had grown up together. He
was a tall fair, fresh-faced youth with a serious core

which somehow set him apart from the other young people in Stevie's circle and made him kin to herself. Over the years they had shared everything— skiing trips, books, a love of jazz, and though their interests at university had diverged somewhat, they had remained close, seeing each other almost daily. Jordan had graduated before her and gone on to do postgraduate work in science at the same university, where he also worked as her father's laboratory assistant. But Stevie had other plans. She wanted to stretch her wings, try her luck in the big city.

'It's not to do with other men,' Stevie had carefully explained to Jordan during one of their increasingly serious talks. 'It's simply that I want to explore a little of the world, find out about my English side.'

Jordan had shrugged. 'We could get married first and then, if I can find a post somewhere in England, we can go over together.'

'Oh, it's too soon to get married!' Stevie had stiffened abruptly.

The cool searching look he had given her remained imprinted on her mind. In response to it, Stevie had said it would be wonderful if he could be in England too. But marriage—no, she didn't feel quite ready somehow. It was all so grown-up, so definitive.

'All right Stevie,' Jordan had agreed, 'but much as I love you, I can't wait for ever.'

It was the first time he had used the word, and Stevie had given him a curious look. Love—the sound of that word too had a finality that made her distinctly uncomfortable.

As it turned out, an English post for Jordan had not been immediately forthcoming, and Stevie had secretly breathed a sigh of relief. And though she assured herself that she missed Jordan and their daily conversations, and she conjured up his name anytime another man's advances became pressing, half of her was well pleased to be quite on her own. Jordan's growing sexual insistence just before her departure was something she could well do without, could happily postpone until the inevitable day arrived. Luckily he had always been too much of a gentleman to press her too far. It was not a part of life that interested her, Stevie assured herself again. And then her eyes flew wide open as she realised where she was and what she had just experienced.

James's strong profile jutted out at her through the shadows. She trembled, half realising her lie to herself.

Feeling her eyes on him, he flashed her a look. 'Sleepy?' She nodded.

He put out an arm to draw her towards him, and she flinched.

'I promise you my shoulder won't violate any vows you may have made.' His tone dripped with irony, and Stevie made herself as small as possible in the far corner of the car. She saw him shrug and she closed her eyes, willing away the magnetism of his presence. Sleep descended on her.

It seemed only seconds later that she had the distinct sensation of a pair of grey-blue eyes surveying her lazily from a great distance, a pair of lips softly caressing her cheek. Her eyes started open. Instantly she realised that she had been fast asleep, that against her waking will, she had cuddled close to James, had been resting her head on his shoulder. His arm was around her and the humorous tilt of his lips betrayed the sultry heaviness of his eyes.

Stevie sat bolt upright. 'I'm sorry,' she murmured. 'The drink must have sent me off to sleep.'

'We've only been here for a few minutes,' he smiled at her embarrassment.

Startled, she looked round and saw that they were parked in front of her flat. She felt awkward, silly, and mumbling a 'thank you for seeing me home,' she made to open the door, wondering simultaneously when she had given him her address.

James was round to her side of the car before she had

completely emerged and she stumbled against him. He put an arm round her to steady her. 'I'll see you up, Stevie. Never let it be said that we Scots aren't gentlemen—at least occasionally!'

Stevie's pulse began to race, as much because of his nearness as because she didn't know how to handle things once they were upstairs. She fumbled for her key and found it just as they reached the flat. James took the key gently from her hand and opened the door for her.

'Thank you,' she said again, still awkward.

'Are you feeling all right?' he asked.

She nodded and looked up into his face.

His eyes beneath the rugged brow seemed to be searching hers.

'I'll see you, then, Stevie,' he said after what seemed an eternity. 'Take care of yourself.'

With the swift, supple movements of a night creature, he was at the stairs and away. Stevie looked confusedly at his receding shape and, too late, called a goodnight after him.

She closed the door of the flat and leant heavily on it for a moment, breathing deeply before switching on the light. With a pang she realised that she had wanted him to come in, to stay a little, to—yes, to kiss her once more.

'I'm being idiotic,' she chided herself, wrapping her arms round her waist. 'Completely idiotic.' With an abrupt gesture she kicked off her shoes sending them flying to the centre of the room, then went into the kitchen. Here she let the tap run for a few moments and then drank down two large glasses of water. 'Drunk, that's what I am,' she told her image in the bathroom mirror, 'and in wine lie all the seeds of romantic fantasy. Tall, dark, ravishingly attractive men who kiss you passionately, with sensual lips and sweep you off your feet.' She laughed aloud, deriding the little gnawing voice within her which dared to whisper—but he did, Stevie, didn't he?

CHAPTER FOUR

STEVIE was late coming into the office that Monday. She felt drained. All her energy seemed to be going into keeping James Reid out of her mind. He had awoken a life in her which she refused to recognise, and keeping it away from the limits of her waking consciousness was proving hard work. As she shuffled through the day's post in a desultory manner, Anthony came in.

'Survived the party, Stevie?' He looked at her quizzically.

'Just,' Stevie answered, making a face. 'And you?'

'I've survived. But my heart!' he clasped his hands to his chest in a dramatic gesture.

'Well, keep your Cupid to yourself,' she said, more irritation evident in her voice than she had intended.

Anthony's eyebrows rose. 'A little touchy today, are we? No bubbly Americanisms, no hurricane-like energies?'

Stevie managed a smile. 'Sorry, Anthony. Woke up on the wrong side of the bed, I guess.'

'As long as you didn't bump into anyone there,' he taunted.

She flung a pencil at him.

'The hurricane begins to gather force,' he grinned.

'It had better,' she sighed. 'All this to get through,' she pointed at the post, 'and James Reid's future to start work on.'

'Lucky man, that one,' Anthony drawled. 'Not only is he talented, but he has two of the most beautiful women in the world working for him.'

'Well, this one isn't working very hard, so do keep quiet, Mr Howell.' Stevie tried to suppress another wave of irritation at the thought of being coupled with Irena. She reached for a large manilla envelope and made a great show of settling down to work, putting off the moment when she would have to start ringing editors on James's behalf. Then, angry at herself, she picked up the phone and began to make appointments with a frenzy, starting with the glossiest mags. Amidst all this she rang her mother at her editorial office. She wanted to check whether her instincts about whom to contact and in what order were correct.

'Mum!' Stevie immediately recognised her mother's soft even tones at the end of her private line.

'Stevie! How have you been keeping, darling? I haven't seen you for an age.'

'You can see me today, if you have a few minutes. I could be there in half an hour.'

'Make it an hour, Stevie, and I'll buy you some lunch.'

'You're an angel, Mum!' Stevie rang off.

She busied herself by rearranging James's photographs into the sequences she liked best, and familiarising herself with the clothes worn in each print and their points of origin.

'Things going well?' Anthony invaded her thoughts.

She crossed her fingers. 'I'm off now.'

She raced down the stairs and covered the few streets to her mother's office in record time.

The magazine had its premises in a large modern building which housed other publications by the same group. Stevie waved to the security man, pressed the lift button for the fifth floor, passed a brush quickly through her hair (her mother insisted on a little tidiness) and sauntered out on to the carpet-covered corridor which led to her mother's office.

'Hello, Anita,' Stevie greeted her mother's secretary. 'Is the taskmaster ready for me?'

'Sh!' Anita's eyes grew large with mock reprimand. 'You'll lose me my job!'

'Little chance of that. You run the place,' Stevie grinnned. Anita had been with her mother for years and Stevie loved teasing her.

'My prodidgal daughter has arrived, has she?' Stevie's mother appeared at the inner office door. 'Can't mistake those hushed New England tones a mile away!' Susannah Henderson looked at her offspring indulgently and came forward to embrace Stevie and plant a kiss on both cheeks.

Just a few inches shorter than Stevie, she looked for all her fifty years more like an older sister than a mother. Her blonde hair pulled back into a loose chignon which sat delicately at the nape of her neck, her trim figure clad in a simple pale grey linen suit every seam of which spelled couture, she had a quiet elegance which never ceased to amaze Stevie, who considered herself something of an expert in these matters.

The two women stepped back to take a good look at each other and smiled the same wide smile of appreciation.

'I don't know how he can bear to be without you,' Stevie said.

'If you mean your father, my little one, he can't. He'll be here in the not-too-distant future.'

'Wonderful!' Stevie exclaimed her delight. 'I can't wait to see him.'

'Just as I can't wait to hear all about you.' Her mother took her by the arm and guided her out of the office. 'And while you're talking, I'll make up for some of my maternal omissions by feeding that ravenous appetite of yours!'

Stevie smiled. Her ability to put down quantities of food was a family joke.

They went to a small quiet restaurant—filled with businessmen communing in hushed tones—a few steps from her mother's office. After they had placed their orders, Susannah Henderson turned an expectant face to her daughter. 'Well?'

'Well, I seem to have my first client for the fashion world, and he's a dilly,' Stevie put on a wry face.

'Troublesome?' her mother quizzed her.

'A little.' Stevie swallowed hard as she thought of James's brooding face and commanding tones. 'But I think I can handle him,' she put assurance into her voice. 'Here, have a look at these,' she passed her mother one of her folders.

Susannah Henderson looked through the photographs quietly and then gestured for Stevie to show her some more. Stevie waited breathlessly for her mother's expert verdict.

Finally she looked away from the photos and up at her daughter. 'Well, my girl, if he can produce these to order, you have yourself a high-flyer. Whom have you approached?'

Stevie went through her list and beamed when her mother approved.

'Make your way through the posh mags first,' Susannah Henderson suggested. 'I think his flair is for those rather than the teenage side of the market, though I imagine this man can do anything he sets his camera to. As long as he's co-operative.'

Before Stevie had a chance to express any doubts on that score, a tall raven-haired woman sporting an impeccable white trouser suit was upon them.

'Susannah darling!' the words dripped honey from her mouth. 'How absolutely divine to bump into you here! How have you been?'

Stevie, who knew her mother's responses well, saw her flinch imperceptibly. But her tone was all charm. 'Bettina, this is a surprise. I didn't know you were in this country.'

'Just here for a flying visit, darling. Otherwise I would have rung to make a date.'

'Stevie, this is Bettina Carnap. My daughter Stevie, Bettina.' Stevie registered the name of the fashion editor of a top New York glossy and was suddenly all ears.

She could see her mother, too, gearing up for action, despite her evident dislike for this woman.

'Sit down for a minute, Bettina. Stevie has been showing me some work by a brilliant new photographer she's handling. Would you like a preview peep? He's about to become all the rage here.'

Bettina Carnap glanced at her watch, looked round the room to check that her lunch date hadn't yet turned up, and edged her long body on to a chair.

'Don't mind if I do, darling.' She cast a haughty dark eye on Stevie, who handed her Reid's photographs. She flicked quickly through the pictures, uttered a breathy, 'Irena Borg! These are good,' and then, without warning, looked Stevie right in the eye. 'Would your man be free to take on an engagement in Scotland in about two weeks' time? I'd arranged for some work to be done at Castle Urquhart and our photographer has fallen through.'

Stevie glanced at her mother, who gave her an imperceptible nod. 'I'll check with him and let you know. His name is James Reid, incidentally.'

'Good, you can contact my assistant and she'll give you all necessary details. She's here for a few weeks.' Bettina handed Stevie a card and rose to go. 'All favours squared, Susannah darling.'

Stevie's mother smiled, 'Have a good stay, Bettina, and let me know when you're next in London.'

Susannah Henderson gave Stevie a slow wink which transformed her elegant fine-boned face into that of a naughty girl. 'Sometime's pays to have lunch with your mother, doesn't it, Stevie?'

'I'll say!' Stevie grinned, ogling the plate of tagliatelle the waiter had just placed in front of her. 'It even has the side benefits of a few business contacts.'

The two women met each other's eyes and laughed as they heard Bettina's echoing 'darling' at the other end of the restaurant.

'Make sure your photographer's up to scratch,

though, Stevie. Bettina may like squaring favours, but she knows her business and he'll have to work to order, as well as use what imagination he has.'

'Don't worry, Mum,' said Stevie, anxiety already mixed with her jubilance as she thought of the difficulties James Reid might pose.

'And now tell me about you. Any new men in your life?'

An image of Reid's dark curly head and rugged face invaded Stevie's mind with palpable force. Colouring a little, she blotted it away and looked at her mother archly. 'Not a single one, Mum. Haven't the time.'

'Still saving yourself for that Jordan Richards?' Susannah's tone was clearly disapproving.

'Oh, Mother, don't start on that! You know how fond I am of Jordan,' Stevie pleaded.

'Yes, yes, being fond is fine,' her mother returned impatiently. 'He's a nice enough youth. But you're a woman now, so don't end up caught in your own safety net, Stevie. You're too good for that.'

Stevie gave her mother a puzzled look, but the older woman simply shrugged and turned the conversation on to less trying ground.

As she answered her queries about work, Stevie thought over her mother's comments about Jordan. Was she really simply using him as a safety net—a first line of defence against the merest possiblity of any other men seriously intervening in her life? Was that all that Jordan meant to her, a bulwark against disturbance? If that was the case she was a coward of the first rank. She remembered how she had conjured up Jordan's presence at the very moment when James's magnetism had become almost too strong to bear. The memory chafed and brought with it a sense of overriding shame. Here she had always prided herself on her moral uprightness, the attention she paid to behaving well, behaving honestly and so as not to hurt people, lead them on. No, she rebelled at the thought; she couldn't simply be using Jordan. She *was* exceedingly fond of him. There was no man she liked as much and she did want to marry him—eventually. Or did she? Again James's image came to her mind and sent her pulse racing.

'Stevie,' her mother's voice penetrated her thoughts, 'I've asked you three times whether you wanted some pudding. The fact that you haven't heard the magic word must mean you're ill!' Susannah's face had a droll expression.

'No, Mum, just growing up. I was thinking about your safety net and got carried away.' Stevie sighed. 'You shouldn't be so perceptive. I think I'll skip the pudding. I should get back to the office.'

Her mother took on a look of exaggerated astonishment. 'You *must* be growing up, little one!' She offered her cheek to Stevie for a kiss. 'Let me know how you get on with your James Reid, and if you need any help, don't hesitate to ask.'

'Thanks, Mum, you're an angel!' Stevie called over her shoulder, meaning it.

As she walked into the office, Jan called out to her.

'Just in time, Stevie. There's a chappie by the name of Tom Brewster on the phone for you.' She gave Stevie a salacious wink. 'Hobnobbing with the boss's clan these days, are you?'

Stevie picked up the telephone by Jan's side and made a gesture of incomprehension.

Tom Brewster's voice was distinct at the other end of the line.

'Hope you're free tonight, Stevie. I thought I might treat you to dinner at the Athenaeum Hotel.'

'That sounds wonderful!' Stevie replied, genuine excitement in her tone. The Athenaeum was one of those places she had only ever heard about but never visited.

'I could pick you up, or meet you there at eight.'

'Let's meet there. I don't know whether I'll manage to get home first.' She rang off and, deliberately shunning Jan's questioning look made for her office. There she decided it was time to familiarise herself with fashion photography fees both in London and the U.S.A., and with the ad agencies which she hadn't previously dealt with in a fashion context. She didn't ring to tell James the news about the American glossy; it would hold until their dinner date tomorrow. She smiled secretly to herself as she thought of his surprised pleasure at the quick results she was getting.

At half past five she decided that she would after all make a quick dash home to change. She didn't get taken to the Athenaeum Hotel every night.

She showered, washed and dried her hair to a gleaming mass and then, humming a perky little tune to herself, she dressed in a creamy white jump suit she had recently bought in a Covent Garden boutique. The suit was trimmed round the shoulders and plunging neck with lavish flounces of old cotton lace and it lightly emphasised the lines of her body, just allowing a glimpse of the firm contours of her breasts. The lace set off her elegant neck and head with a dash of playful romanticism. She donned a contrasting emerald belt, blithely put on a little make-up and then went out to catch a taxi. It deposited her outside the grey stone façade of the hotel, and holding her head high so as not to let her excitement show, Stevie walked past the doorman into the discreetly-lit lobby.

All reserve and quiet elegance, she noted to herself, as she let her eyes drift round the room. It was the scale that did it, as much as anything else. No mammoth ostentation here.

'Hello, Stevie,' Tom Brewster's voice suprised her from behind. She turned to catch his eyes raking over her wickedly. 'You look positively delicious! The chef will have to work very hard to get any of my attention.' He fingered the lace round her throat, letting his fingers graze her skin accidentally in the process.

Stevie suddenly felt decidedly uncomfortable. Perhaps she should have refused Tom's invitation. 'It's lovely here,' she said inconsequentially to hide her embarrassment.

'Yes, it is,' he pushed her remark aside, his eyes still lingering on her face. 'Shall we have a drink first? Our table is booked for eight forty-five.'

Stevie nodded and he passed his arm round her waist to guide her towards the hotel bar. They were shown to a quiet corner and she tried to relax into the deep armchairs. It passed through her mind that apart from making her jittery, Tom Brewster's touch made no impact on her whatsoever. Not like Mr Genghis Khan, she thought bitterly.

It was almost as if the vagrant thought had conjured him up, for Tom suddenly exclaimed, 'Why, there's Tara Alexander, and I do believe she's with that photographer you deal with—what's his name? I told you it was a small world!'

Stevie blanched. Coming directly towards them were James and a dramatically dark woman clothed in a sumptuous magenta silk dress which swung rhythmically round her hips and set off the almost theatrical darkness of her features.

For someone who pretends to be something of a misogynist, James Reid, Stevie muttered to herself, you certainly do get around! She swallowed hard as she looked at him. The quiet distinction of his light suit gave him a kind of lazy grace which made him more dangerously attractive than ever. She found her eyes straying across the broad expanse of his chest, the muscular length of his legs, taut against the fabric of his trousers.

He raked a hand through the dark, curly tangle of his hair and his blue-grey eyes met hers. 'Hello, Stevie,' he murmured, beneath the louder resonance of the woman's voice.

'Tom Brewster—I don't believe it! It's been years!'

Tom rose to embrace her warmly. 'And you're as devastating as ever, Tara. Do join us.' He looked at James, who nodded and pulled up two chairs to their table, and introduced Stevie to Tara Alexander.

The dark woman looked at Stevie with evident curiosity before stretching out a hand. 'Is this young lady a friend of yours as well, James?' she asked. 'I must say your women do seem to get younger and younger!'

'Now, Tara, stop trying to accuse me of cradle-snatching! Stevie Henderson is quite old enough to take care of herself, I can assure you.' James looked at Stevie meaningfully and then glanced reflectively at Tom Brewster. 'In any case, she's my agent, and our dealings are altogether professional.' A mocking light came into his eyes, 'Isn't that so, Stevie?'

'Quite decidedly so,' Stevie replied coldly, and added under her breath for James's ears alone, 'and I intend to keep them that way.' She noticed the icy look that spread over James features, but she turned her gaze innocently away and asked Tom, 'Are you and Tara *very* old friends?'

'As old as the hills,' Tom laughed her intent aside, warmly enveloping the group in an expansive gesture. 'And certainly old enough to know that the lady only ever drinks champagne before dinner.' He signalled to the waiter.

Before Stevie knew it, she was drinking champagne, its fragrant bubbles tickling her nose. It was only when Tara and Tom were well launched into one of those 'and whatever became of so-and-so' conversations that she allowed her eyes to meet James's again.

He had been relatively quiet while the others chatted, but Stevie had been so acutely aware of his presence, that her skin seemed to tingle with a strange electricity. Now, as she looked at him directly, she recognised the sardonic tilt to his lips.

'You've quite survived the other evening's party, I

see, Stevie, and once again forgotten this trusting flame of yours back home. The sensuous luxuries of life do have a way of predominating.' His eyes, like tempered steel, observed her disapprovingly.

'My flames, trusting or not, have nothing to do with you, James Reid!' Stevie retorted angrily. This man had a distinct way of kindling her temper.

He reached slowly into his jacket pocket for a cigarette and she followed the movement of his hand as if mesmerised, her eyes taking in the tautness of his limbs, the flatness of his stomach beneath his shirt, the muscular grace of his hand as he struck a match.

His eyebrows arched devilishly as he caught her look, 'Yes, I know, our dealings are totally professional. As professional as your dealings with Tom Brewster, I have no doubt.'

Stevie met him on it. 'No, far more professional. Tom is a friend.'

'I see.' He eyed her quizzically for a moment and then with a change of expression raised his glass to her provocatively. 'Shall we drink to varieties of friendship, then, Stevie? Perhaps we could experiment with a few.'

'What are you two plotting?' Tara Alexander caught the shared challenge of their look.

'James Reid's working life,' Stevie answered boldly, surprised at her own mendacity.

'Not the book!' Tara exclaimed. James glared at her. 'Oh, darling, have I let the cat out of the bag? I'm so sorry—I won't breathe another word.' Adeptly she changed the subject, though Stevie knew Tara wasn't in the least sorry. She had scored her point, brought into play private knowledge about James which Stevie certainly didn't have.

The waiter arrived to tell Tom that their table was ready, and loath though she was to leave Tara and James alone together, Stevie managed to bid them a polite enough goodbye. At the last moment she remembered that she and James were meant to meet for dinner the following evening. Her heart sank as she thought that perhaps her behaviour tonight might have alienated him completely. With an uncustomary boldness she called over her shoulder, 'Don't forget that I'm picking you up for dinner around eight tomorrow. Donne and Brewster believe in treating their clients well!'

'Do they now?' James met her eyes. 'We'll see about that . . .'

As she and Tom walked through to the restaurant, Stevie was barely aware of her surroundings. She had swallowed Tara's bait. What book was James involved in? Her mind began to circle round James, all the things she didn't know about him, the reasons he had given up war photography, the reasons for his sudden re-appearance in London. She was almost oblivious to the sumptuous dinner—the delicacy of the *timbales d'asperges*, the pale pink salmon cooked to a turn, the rich creamy chocolate mousse that all but floated in her mouth.

Luckily Tom's conversation was light and unde-manding, and she could laugh at his stories while part of her pondered the enigma of James Reid, this man who had come into her life so recently, but who seemed to colour it altogether. He continued to colour it even as Tom drove her home in the elegant white Mercedes he had borrowed from his sister-in-law for the duration of his stay in England; even as he kissed her lightly on the lips before she slid away from his arms, politely thanked him for a delightful evening and promised to see him before he returned to Brazil, if time permitted.

James Reid occupied the centre of her thoughts, and she had not even a passing pang of guilt vis-à-vis Jordan, the man, she had reassured herself earlier that day, she was prepared to spend her life with.

The next morning Stevie dressed carefully in a light beige linen suit and a green blouse that matched her

eyes. She looked, her image told her, coolly sophisticated—just what was needed for a day packed with
meetings with fashion editors. She popped into the
office only for a moment to pick up the files containing
James's prints, and found Anthony humming to himself
exuberantly.

When he saw her, he whirled her round the room in a
madcap dance.

Stevie groaned. 'Where's the sensible, intelligent man
I used to know?'

'He's in hiding for a few days.' Anthony's brown eyes
were luminous. 'Guess what? I've dared to ask her out
and she's said yes!'

For a moment Stevie wasn't sure whom he meant.
'Irena?' she finally asked.

Anthony nodded.

'But that's wonderful!' Stevie exclaimed, infected by
his good humour. With a little inner grimace, she
realised that she was pleased for more reasons than
one.

'Wish me luck. I'm off to brave the fashion world.'

'All the luck in the world,' Anthony called after her.
'Not that anyone will be able to resist the package of
you *and* Reid!'

Stevie walked briskly to her first appointment, and it
was indeed as if she had been blessed by a fairy
godmother. The fashion editor was thrilled with James's
prints, doubly thrilled because they were by him. What
she wanted was a photo feature accompanied by an
interview with James. It was only when she had left the
magazine office that it occurred to Stevie that Reid
might resist the interview. He wasn't altogether
forthcoming about his private life.

Stevie shrugged away her doubts and boarded a bus
that would take her to her next meeting. The day
hummed with activity, an endless round of persuasive
chat which ended with several more distinct possibilities
for James. By the end of the afternoon, she felt she had

more than earned her keep, and she made her way home jubilantly.

But as she showered and changed a nervousness overtook her. What on earth did she think she was doing, having dinner with this Genghis Khan of a man who invaded her senses, her thoughts, as no man had ever done? It really wasn't called for in the line of duty. She suddenly thought of her mother's term—the safety net—and she conjured up Jordan's fresh-faced image. She wondered whether her mother would agree with her that perhaps in this particular instance, the safety net was necessary, a protection against the dizzying heights which James Reid seemed so casually to sweep her up into. This time, Mum, she pleaded, there's a real danger, a real man, a throwback, a Genghis Khan, a man who's survived a decade of the women's movement unscathed. I need my safety net—need it desperately, or I'll fall off the tightrope, like Irena, like heaven knows how many others.

Stevie shivered and started to dial James's number. She would call off the meeting and simply relate to him what she had managed to achieve. But when she had finished dialling the number, she hung up. She was being silly. She couldn't spend her days hiding from him. And if her feeling for Jordan was strong enough, it would carry her through. No mere physical impulse could overcome that, she assured herself.

She tried to quiet her inner voices and concentrate on dressing. She put on a tawny brown dress with a wide flounced skirt and full sleeves and wrapped a wide soft belt twice round her waist. Then she set off rapidly, before any more self-reflection could stop her. She deliberately focussed her thoughts on what it was she wanted to find out about James Reid; like a private eye, she laughed to herself, hot on the track of the missing years of James Reid's life. Tonight, she promised herself, he wouldn't evade her questions.

As she rang the now familiar bell, she felt strangely

lightheaded. There was no immediate answer, so she rang again, thinking that perhaps she hadn't pressed hard enough the first time. Still no one appeared, and Stevie glanced at her watch. No, she was right on time. Perhaps James had forgotten their engagement. Her heart skipped a beat and she was about to turn away, when the door opened.

She was totally unprepared for what confronted her: James Reid stood there in a bright blue, loosely tied, towelling robe, his legs and tousled hair still dripping with water.

'Sorry, I miscalculated by some ten minutes.' There was a mischievous smile on his face as his eyes, large and breathtakingly blue beneath their thick wet lashes, surveyed her lazily. 'Come on up.'

He stood back so that Stevie could precede him through the door, and as she brushed past him she was acutely aware of his nakedness beneath the robe. It sent a flush into her cheeks and a troubled pounding through her veins. He gestured her towards the staircase she had never before climbed, and nervously she mounted the narrow stairs, every part of her sensitive to the presence immediately behind her.

'Through there,' he pointed her towards a door. 'Fix yourself a drink. I'll be right back.'

Stevie found her eyes focussing, despite herself, on the dark curly hair that escaped his robe. He caught her at it and his smile grew even more mischievous. Abruptly he passed a finger down the smooth line of her cheek. 'That way,' the caressing finger now pointed towards the door behind her while his voice mocked gently.

Stevie turned and walked into a large airy room. She felt she had suddenly woken from a deep hypnosis and moving towards an open window, she took a long breath. Terrible, the effect this man has on me, she told a row of small neat gardens just beginning to burgeon into flowery life. I guess this is what they call the force of attraction, she shook her head comically. Watch your mind and your manners, Stevie Henderson; this is meant to be a work meeting.

She turned now and looked round the room, taking in its detail. A bachelor's den, she thought to herself. One end held a neat well-equipped kitchen separated from the rest of the space by a pine counter. A round pine table occupied the space next to one window. She was surprised at the large bowl of purple and blue flowers at its centre and she chided her own surprise: comic book ideas of what men did and didn't do. At the other end of the room two low cream-coloured sofas occupied a corner. A long pine coffee table stood in front of them. Some easy chairs, richly decorated rugs on a highly polished floor, a stereo and masses of records, and on the walls, drawings which even to Stevie's unpractised eyes looked good completed the impression of air and space. A comfortable informal room, she decided, liking it. She began to relax a little.

But before she had a chance to do so properly, James was back, well-washed denims hugging his long muscular legs, a checked blue and white open-necked shirt loosely covering his powerful shoulders, his hair still wet and tousled and the mischievous grin still playing over his face. He didn't look as if he were in the least ready for a professional dinner date.

'What, no drink yet?' His eyes caressed her goodhumouredly. 'Did my semi-undress send you into a state of virginal shock?'

Stevie gulped. 'Certainly not! I was just—well, surprised.'

'As should all well brought up New England young ladies be at such moments.' There was a distinct twinkle in his eye, Stevie noted. He was laughing at her, but she let it pass, unwilling to take this part of the conversation any further.

He walked towards the fridge and took out a bottle of white wine which he uncorked. Without asking her what she wanted, he handed her a glass. 'It will settle you,' he explained, leaning his tall frame against the counter. Then he looked at her provocatively. 'And have you any business news to relay to me, Ms Super-Agent? A little jaunt to the sands of the Sahara? Or perhaps a modelling spree on the Acropolis?'

'Nothing quite so grand,' Stevie replied, 'but I do have some business news.'

His evident surprise pleased her and restored a little of her equanimity. She reached for the file she had carefully labelled 'James Reid' and drew out a sheet of paper.

James shook his head whimsically. 'That's my fate—reduced to a file in the care of an altogether professional lady!'

'Not such a very bad fate, as you'll see,' Stevie bantered back. 'I've got you an assignment with a top American mag. In Scotland the week after next, if you can manage it.'

'Manage it!' He whisked her up in his arms and twirled her round the room. 'I'd trade three trips to the Sahara for one assignment in Scotland these days. How did you guess?'

Stevie untangled herself from his arms. She was all too overwhelmingly aware of the lingering scent of his aftershave, the firm contours of his back beneath the light cotton of his shirt, and she lowered her eyes away from him. She couldn't stay in this intimate space with him.

'Shall we go out for that dinner now and celebrate?' she said as lightly as she could.

He shook his head. 'I couldn't face the thought of your entertaining me, as you put it so blithely, so I've cooked us some dinner here.'

Stevie's face fell.

'I'm not such a bad cook as all that. Living alone has its educative value,' he teased, and pointing her towards a chair, busied himself with setting the table.

Stevie tried to restore her composure by assuming a businesslike tone again. 'There's more to report,' she said.

'I'm all ears.' He placed a dish of pâté and some gherkins on the table, pulled a hot loaf out of the oven and sat down beside her.

'The other definite assignment has a condition attached to it.'

'Everything in life has conditions attached to it, Stevie.' His eyes held hers for a moment and she could feel her pulse beginning to race. The sensation made her angry with herself and the words stumbled out of her bluntly.

'This mag wants to do an interview with you to accompany the photo spread. You know the kind of thing, "Intrepid war photographer turns his camera to fashion"'

Like a lightning bolt, James was out of his chair and towering over her. 'Most definitely not.' He turned to pace the room, a scowl on his face. 'I won't do it,' he said coldly. 'Don't you Americans have any tact? Any sense of privacy?'

Stevie bridled, 'Why ever not? You'll get free publicity. All the fashion editors will be asking for you.'

He looked at her contemptuously. 'I'm not in this to be a star.'

Stevie persisted, despite her better judgement. 'One article will hardly make you a star. But it will help me get you more work—which is, after all, what we want.'

'Not that way. I don't want some nosey journalist prying into my life, turning me into what I'm not,' he hissed out between gritted teeth.

'Well, if you have so much to hide.' The words were out before Stevie could stop them.

He turned on her, his eyes two narrow slits above the prominent cheekbones. 'I have nothing to hide, Ms Super-Agent. But I am not about to become fodder for the media hounds. I know them too well. I've worked with them for a good part of my life and they've already dined on me quite enough.'

Stevie shrugged. 'Fine, if that's the way you want it, we'll just drop that assignment. But you know,' she met his eyes boldly, 'they're bound to write about you sooner or later. You're an interesting subject. Not every war photographer turns to the glittering world of fashion.'

He shot her a look of such pure hatred that Stevie suddenly began to tremble. 'Well, you know it's true,' she said softly, and, ready to burst into tears, rose, and gathered her file together clumsily.

'Sit down, Stevie.' The controlled rage in Reid's voice made her stop dead in her tracks. 'Please sit down,' he said again, more gently. He filled her glass. 'You're right, of course, it's bound to happen sooner or later, so I might as well get it over with.' He took a long gulp of wine and suddenly looked at her reflectively. A smile began to hover round his lips. 'What if you did the interview?'

'Me?' Stevie eyed him uncomprehendingly. 'I can't do that!'

'Why not? I'll talk to you, and I trust you not to pry *too* much or distort what I say.'

'It wouldn't be ethical,' Stevie grabbed at excuses. 'I'm your agent, after all.'

'I shouldn't imagine your magazine will have quite so refined a conscience. Try it on them, see what they say. And now let's think of other things,' he passed her the bowl of pâté. 'In any case, once the Scottish feature is done, there shouldn't be any lack of work. The offers will come flooding in and I can begin to do some experimenting.'

Stevie was a little dismayed at his certainty, suddenly too, a little afraid that he might not need her then. 'Don't you think that's a little over-confident of you?' she asked querulously.

James looked at her harshly and then smiled again.

'Yes, far too arrogant. But I know what I can do. In any case, another six to eight months of this and I won't need to do more than the occasional fashion feature.'

Stevie's astonishment showed in her face. She looked at the man opposite her, the strong handsome face with its clear gaze. He caught her eyes on him and raised his glass to her. 'If you don't stop looking at me like that, we won't get to the next course! And this is supposed to be a professional meeting, as you insisted yesterday,' his smile teased her.

Stevie pushed a hand a little nervously through the heavy gold of her hair, sweeping it away from her face. 'I was just wondering about you,' she said.

'No more than I wonder about you.' Gently he lifted a strand of hair from her face and threw it back. He gazed at her reflectively as she flinched away from his touch and then the mockery came back into his eyes. 'But there isn't room for any of that if we're to carry on in a businesslike fashion . . . under your orders.'

Stevie lowered her eyes from the assault of his and said the first thing that came into her mind. 'I should let you know that I have a monstrous appetite.'

'For food, I suppose you mean,' he teased again, and Stevie could feel the colour beginning to steel into her cheeks. Before she could reply he had placed a fragrant casserole on the table, pork chops in a creamy basil and mustard sauce, a second dish of parsleyed potatoes, and a bowlful of crisp salad. He served her silently, poured some more wine, and only when he sat down did he speak again.

'I'm sorry if I barked at you before.' He reached for her hand, but Stevie drew it away. James groaned exaggeratedly. 'It's my Ghenghis Khan temper, as you once called it.' He laughed at himself. 'I can't stand the idea of journalists invading my life—perhaps because I worked with them for so long. I have this fetish, this "thing", as you Americans call it, about privacy.'

'I wish you'd stop treating my Americanness as some sort of disease,' Stevie said morosely. 'I am half English, you know.'

'That's hardly a recommendation for a Scot.' A smile travelled from his eyes to his lips, warming his face and enveloping her. Stevie felt a tremor pass through her. 'Now tell me about yourself, Ms Super-Agent. Why are you in London and not, say, in New York?'

Stevie explained about her father and her mother, about her long-time interest in photography. After initial hesitation, she found herself talking easily, answering James's numerous questions with her usual good humour, the comic self-send-ups which were so characteristic of her. 'And that's how I came to London to see the Queen and work for Genghis Khan,' Stevie finished drolly. 'A sad and sorry destiny.'

'And this man of yours is waiting patiently for you back home?' James asked casually.

Stevie put her knife and fork down firmly. 'Now, Mr Reid, you're about to cross the bounds of *my* sense of privacy,' she pronounced the word with a short 'i' and looked up at him, her green eyes wide and sparkling. 'In any case, it's your turn. Tell me about *yourself*, Mr Reid. How did you really happen to come into the fashion world?'

He passed her the salad bowl. 'All will be revealed, Ms Stevie Super-Agent, when you carry out your momentous interview. And that will be on native ground. In Scotland. Did I tell you I'd decided you were coming with me?'

Stevie all but choked on the wine she was swallowing. 'What on earth are you talking about?' Her voice emerged in a high-pitched squeak.

'You heard me. Claude won't be able to come. He has some of his own work to do, and I need an assistant. You know all about cameras, so why not?'

'But,' Stevie protested, 'There's work, and Mr Brewster . . .'

'Oh, I'll arrange that, not to worry. I'm sure he'll be happy to have you accompany me. In any case, I need someone to protect me from all those terribly aggressive American women.' He looked at her sardonically.

She was about to pounce on his remark when he caught her hand and held it firmly. 'That was a joke, Stevie, a half-joke in any case.' He forced her gaze to his and she met the challenge of his eyes. 'You will come, won't you?'

She wrenched her hand away. It was beginning to catch fire from his touch and send little alarming messages coursing through her body.

'I'll think about it,' she said, standing up. 'But right now, I'd better go.' She glanced at her watch without seeing the time.

'No coffee? No cheese or fruit? Stevie,' his voice chided her and in one swift movement he was at her side. 'Stevie,' this time his voice was lower and seemed to catch in mid-breath. He grasped her face with both his hands and forcing her to look up at him, pushed his fingers through the lush thickness of her hair. She met his smouldering glance as he bent her head backwards and suddenly his lips claimed hers with an urgency that sent her heart pounding madly.

'Don't,' she murmured when his mouth left hers to graze over her eyelids, caress her neck with a gentleness which made her body turn liquid.

'Stop me, if you want to.' His lips were in her hair and their mocking murmur sent tremors of such strength through her that she realised that even had she wanted to, her limbs would not have obeyed. She swayed against him, her arms winding themselves round his back, following their own course as they embraced the hardness of his taut muscles and reached round his neck to finger the curly texture of his hair.

He groaned and crushed his mouth to hers. His hands pressed the small of her back, bringing her tightly against him, so that she felt her breasts arch against him with a life of their own. A molten wave passed through her, enveloping her senses, tugging at the pit of her stomach, and she moaned softly.

'Come.' He caught her up in his arms and she was powerless to resist his strength or the blazing glance beneath his heavy, lowered lids. She snuggled against him, winding her arms round his neck, her hands finding the smooth skin beneath his collar. He opened a door and in the moonlight that glistened through the window, Stevie made out a large bed, covered in deepest blue. James laid her on it gently and stretched out beside her. With a featherlight touch, he unfastened the buttons of her shirt and laid her skin bare to his burning gaze. Delicately he traced the line of her throat. A shudder passed through her as his curly head found its way to the hollow between her breasts and she pressed tightly against him. His lips set up a current in her that guided her hands to the satin smoothness of his skin beneath his shirt, to the rougher texture of hair on his chest. With a moan he arched the strong column of his neck, and her lips thirstily caressed its sinewy lines. By some magic, her body matched its rhythm to his, so that when their mouths met again, a simultaneous stifled cry escaped from both at once. Stevie could no longer tell whose limbs belonged to whom, whose heart was beating with a deafening clamour. A flame of pure feeling shot through her, burning away the last remnants of a consciousness which distinguished time, place, self and not self, as she rode on wave after wave of sensation.

At first she thought the bell must be a ringing in her own ears, the shrill echo of her own pulse. But as James moved away from her with a groan, she recognised its insistent distinctness. 'Oh God, I'd forgotten,' his voice was a hoarse whisper. 'I'm sorry, Stevie, dreadfully sorry.' He raised himself to his knees, his eyes still caressing her, and gently he fastened the buttons of her shirt, letting his fingers trail over her pulsing skin. Then, with a swift movement, he was up and out of the room without another word.

Confused, Stevie lay there for a moment trying to gather up her wits. She suddenly felt desolate, as if she'd been abandoned at the bottom of a dark lonely abyss, which had seemed by some optical illusion to be a warm, sun-filled hilltop. Her fingers ran over the crumpled bedcover and with a shiver she sat up.

I've been saved by the proverbial bell, she tried to joke to herself as she straightened her clothes. But the pounding of her senses made it a poor joke. She knew herself well enough to realise that if James had wanted it, she would have succumbed to him without even a second's hesitation. Because his wish would have echoed hers. But obviously he didn't, or the bell would have gone unanswered, she jumped to conclusions. And Jordan? she had completely forgotten him, she thought quietly. And love? the word reared its unwanted presence. She forced it out of her mind. Love could only exist *between* two people, she had always told herself. It wasn't, she had argued with the books and with her friends, anything akin to that transitory sensation of being 'in love', which had more to do with obsesssive imaginings, with sexual compulsions, than with the realities of life. Or so it had always seemed to her in the past.

She shrugged her shoulders, unable to make sense either of her thoughts or her emotions. What was clear was that her knees were wobbly, her hands trembling, a fact that emerged all too clearly as she fumbled with a lamp switch. She heard voices in the drawing room and wanting to escape them she chose another door that led into a bathroom. She poured cold water over her face and finding a comb, passed it through her tangled hair. Her eyes in the mirror above the sink were wide and strangely bright, her cheeks glowing, her lips red. If the mirror could have spoken, it would have talked of a new beauty in her face, but Stevie wasn't prepared to hear. Instead she made her way back to the bedroom, cast a scathing glance at the bed and was about to march out when a woman's voice gave her pause.

She recognised it immediately: Tara Alexander. The rat! Stevie murmured under her breath. The lousy rat! He could take his precious photographs and his precious models and his women and throw them and himself into the sea! With a violent gesture she flung a pillow across the room.

The woman's voice went on, 'It's a wonderful contract, James, absolutely super! You can give up all this silly fasion work and finish the book.'

With as much noise as she could possibly make, Stevie opened the door and stepped into the room.

'I didn't know you had company, James. Still burning both ends of the candle, I see.' Tara's resonant laugh made Stevie's skin crawl. She met James's eyes, and they caressed her languorously. Stevie was enraged that his look should set her pulses throbbing even now. She flashed him a scathing glance as he held a glass up for her.

'Some wine, Stevie?'

She shook her head so violently that her hair tumbled over her face. 'I'm off now,' she announced definitively. 'I hope the book is simply wonderful, James—that it means you can stop doing this silly fashion work, stop dealing with silly people like me.'

James looked at her oddly, surprised at her tone. Then with a quiet authority, he said, 'Wait a little while, Stevie, I'll run you back.'

'No, I must go.' She picked her file up from the table.

'Oh, let the child go, James.' Tara put a proprietorial hand on his arm. 'Her mother will probably be waiting up for her, worrying.'

'I do not live with my mother,' Stevie asserted coldly, and turning on her heel before she burst into tears, she ran down the stairs.

'Stevie.' James was right behind her and he put out a restraining hand as she reached the door.

'Don't touch me!' Stevie's voice snaked out of her.

James dropped his hand at her tone. 'I'll take you back in a little while,' he said grimly.

'No!' she countered, a note of desperation entering her voice as she looked at that ruggedly handsome face. 'I've had enough of this. Just leave me alone!'

His face turned white with rage. 'All right, Stevie, behave like a child, if that's what you want to be.' With controlled precision he opened the door for her.

She walked quickly away not daring to look back.

So James would now not need to do any silly fashion photography, she mimicked Tara's voice to herself. Nor would he need her. She stopped the tears which were mounting to her eyes. 'Good!' she declared aloud. Noticing a taxi coming towards her, she hailed it and leaned well back into the seat. She didn't really want to be part of the Reid harem, she assured herself, prepared at his merest whim to provide him with any kind of service. The word shocked her as she realised its full implications and brought a slightly hysterical giggle to her lips.

'Had a nice evening, miss?' the taxi driver asked, hearing her laugh.

'An illuminating evening,' Stevie replied. 'Wonderfully illuminating. I've learned all about the dangers of male charm,' And to herself she added, 'As well as female duplicity!'

CHAPTER FIVE

STEVIE'S sleep that night was troubled, racked with dreams of tunnels and suffocation. She woke at dawn and lay there tossing amidst clammy sheets. Beyond anything else, she was angry at herself, enraged at her traitorous body which clamoured for James's touch, despite all the dictates of good sense and loyalty. It had betrayed her just as she had betrayed Jordan. It would have betrayed her further, but for the coincidence of a bell.

She dragged herself to work and went about it desultorily, fixing up the details of the Scottish assignment, getting James a larger fee than she had thought possible, and much to her surprise, easily receiving permission to carry out the interview with James herself. She kept waiting for him to ring, but when he hadn't by Friday, she gave up all hope.

Well, that was a very brief fling, she thought to herself, trying to sound wry and grown up, but knowing that she was desolate.

On Saturday morning, hearing Marissa's movements in the next room, she got up and dragged herself towards the kitchen where Marissa was brewing coffee, She hugged her younger sister and then took a long look at her. 'I don't know!' she shook her head maternally. 'I leave you for just a few days and come back to find you looking like the lone survivor of a natural disaster! What on earth has happened?'

'Natural disaster is probably the best way of putting it.' Stevie tried to sound humorous.

Marissa handed her a mug of steaming coffee and eyed her sister quizzically. 'Want to sit down and talk about it?'

'There's nothing much to talk about,' Stevie said bleakly.

Marissa gestured for her sister to sit down beside her and waited expectantly for her to speak. When Stevie remained silent, Marissa began to make small talk. 'France was wonderful. Just wait until you taste the croissants and brioches I've brought back! Whoops, burnt croissants!' Marissa jumped up and came back seconds later with a basketful of flaky pastries. She buttered a croissant for Stevie and dabbed it with jam.

Stevie let the golden crescent rest on its plate. Her sister watched her astutely.

'Stevie, if you don't start eating, I'll have to conclude you're in love!'

Stevie started, her eyes wide with shock.

'Sorry, hon,' Marissa took in her sister's look, 'I thought I was joking. You're not really in love, are you?' she pursued in a low voice.

'Of course not,' Stevie said a little too emphatically, and reaching for a croissant, took a large bite with exaggerated enthusiasm.

'But . . .' Marissa insisted.

'But nothing.' Stevie swallowed the bread, almost choking on it.

'Is it this photographer? I did warn you about him, Stevie.'

Stevie knew better than to lie to her sister. 'He's an attractive man, that's all,' she flushed.

Marissa met her sister's eyes and gazed into them reflectively.

'And difficult?' she prodded.

Stevie nodded and lowered her eyes to her plate.

'Oh, Stevie,' Marissa burst into laughter, 'that's wonderful! I was beginning to lose hope.'

'What do you mean?' Stevie looked at her sister askance.

'Oh, you know. You're so uninterested in men, it's

not—well, natural. And this Jordan of yours is hardly
Mr Right.'

'Jordan's lovely,' Stevie leapt to his defence.

'Yes, yes,' Marissa said impatiently, 'but that has
nothing to do with it.'

'What on earth do you mean?' Stevie asked angrily.

'Oh, Stevie, don't be so naïve! You know he's never
made any real impression on you, really touched you—
inside yourself. And that's what it's all about finally.
Life's not really worth much without that.'

'If you say so,' Stevie muttered. It was not something
she wanted to discuss. 'But I'm not like you,' she added.

Marissa was silent for a moment and then rose to pour
out more coffee. 'I know you disapprove of me, Stevie,
but at least I'm not afraid to live. And even that all-time
hero writer of yours, Henry James, managed to say at
some point, late in life though it was, that one should live,
"live all you can!" Dreadful puritan though he was.'

Stevie's eyes blazed. 'Just like me, you mean.'

Marissa shrugged. 'No, not quite like you. You enjoy
most things too much. But in some areas, younger
sister, you do have the most remarkable set of defences
against life.'

Her sister's comment irritated Stevie. 'Well, at least I
don't go around leading men on and then hurting
them!' she lunged out.

'What on earth are you talking about, Stevie?'
Marissa sounded exasperated.

'You know very well! You told me yourself there was
this youth who trailed after you, whom you felt guilty
about.'

Marissa shrugged. 'That was a long time ago. Look,
Stevie, I know you don't approve of my ways. But at
least I don't hang on to one man childishly, pretending
that I'd be happy to spend my life with him when I
don't even think of him from one moment to the next.
That's no particular justification for acting so high and
mighty.'

Stevie stood up and made to leave the room. Usually the two sisters steered clear of the subject of men. Stevie knew it was silly of her to disapprove of the way Marissa seemed to be constantly surrounded by suitors, to flit in and out of relationships with a casualness totally foreign to her younger sister. But she hadn't known until now how strongly Marissa felt about her relationship with Jordan. It was almost as if she were in league with her mother.

'Stevie!' Marissa's voice called her back, trying to tease her into good humour. 'If I really thought you were becoming susceptible to another man, I'd eat this whole basket of croissants!'

Stevie turned. 'Under your tutelage, Marissa, anything can happen.'

Marissa reached for a croissant and with a groan in answer to Stevie's unvoiced challenge, she took a large bite of the flaky bread.

Stevie watched her sister. 'Keep eating, Marissa, I'm becoming more susceptible by the minute!'

She went to her room and pulled on an old tee-shirt and some well-washed denims. With a pretence of reading, she lay down on the bed. But the incidents of the past week pursued her, filled her with confusion, and suddenly she felt she wanted to share some of the burden with Marissa. After all, her sister was older, wiser, certainly more experienced. And her comments about Jordan rankled. Stevie made another pot of coffee and with a conciliatory gesture handed a cup to Marissa.

Her sister smiled. 'So you've been seeing your photographer regularly, have you?'

'Not *my* photographer,' Stevie insisted, still querulous.

'And what's happened?' Marissa prodded her.

'Nothing.'

'Nothing?' Marissa's voice rose. 'Nothing makes you drag yourself around like some damaged, blank-eyed robot? Come on, Stevie, out with it. Did he sweep you off your feet only to drop you on your bottom with a thud, or worse, did he really do nothing?' She examined her sister's face carefully.

'No, none of those. It's just that I . . . well, I almost slept with him,' Stevie coloured as she brought it out.

'How absolutely dreadful!' Marissa's eyes grew wide in mock consternation. 'How frightfully unnatural!'

'Oh, Marissa, it's not funny!' A pleading note came into Stevie's voice. 'You know I'm not casual about these things.'

Marissa patted Stevie's shoulder. 'I know, I'm only teasing. But out with the rest. Are you sorry you didn't or sorry you got that far in the first place?'

'He doesn't care about me.' Stevie looked at her sister tearfully. 'It just happened. And I—no, my body wanted it to. He . . . he turns me on.' She said the words strangely, as if the expression had never found its place on her lips before.

Marissa started to giggle and then, seeing her sister's look, stopped herself and arranged her face into seriousness. 'You know, Stevie,' she said reflectively, 'your body isn't some kind of abstract entity quite distinct from the rest of you.' She pointed to Stevie's head and heart.

'Well, it feels like that,' Stevie said decidedly.

'Really?' Marissa's gaze penetrated her. 'You mean you don't like this James Reid at all, or even think he's an interesting man?'

'That's not the point,' Stevie felt herself getting into a muddle.

'Then the point is the other way round. He doesn't think—or so you assume—that you're anything more than just a pretty, willing face.' Marissa was being ruthlessly clear, Stevie felt, looking at her sister with something akin to hatred.

Suddenly Marissa laughed gleefully. 'Stevie's in love and won't admit it. Stevie's in love and won't admit it!' she chanted in a playful child's voice.

Stevie grabbed a cushion from the sofa and flung it at her.

'Sorry Stevie,' Marissa looked at her shamefacedly. 'I couldn't help it. You know, there's nothing I can say or do that will provide any consolation. But listen—for your own sake, stop trying to make sense of everything at each and every turn. You worry everything to death!'

'He's asked me—ordered me to come up to Scotland with him on an assignment,' Stevie offered bleakly.

'Well go, you loon, it'll do you a world of good.'

Stevie groaned. 'But I behaved dreadfully and he's probably changed his mind. And what about Jordan?' It all came out in a tumble.

Marissa shrugged. 'You'll have to sort out your guilts for yourself. I know what I'd do.'

'But you're not me,' Stevie said emphatically.

'No,' Marissa answered evenly. 'I jump right into life, rather than pretending it's not there offering irresistible temptations.'

'Whatever the consequences?' Stevie asked.

'Far better that than the regret of not having experienced anything—except the tepid warmth of a security blanket, like your Jordon.'

'That's not fair!' Stevie exclaimed angrily.

'No, but fairness has never been one of my striking characteristics,' Marissa answered. 'I leave you to reflect on it, little sister. Grant's taking me up to Oxford and I have to get ready.'

'Grant?' Stevie queried.

'Yes,' Marissa said emphatically. 'Don't go all disapproving and pretend you've never heard his name before.' Stevie was about to speak, when her sister cut her off. 'And don't worry, he's not one of my young and defenceless admirers. So I won't ruin his life.'

The two sisters looked at each other tensely for a long moment. Then, feeling ashamed, Stevie rose and hugged Marissa. 'Sorry—I'm in a foul temper.'

Marissa's face broke into a smile. 'Never mind, hon,

it'll pass. And if you take it from me, this James Reid sounds a perfect man for you. It'll wake you up a little.'

Stevie groaned. 'You sound more and more like an agony auntie everyday, Marissa!'

'My secret vocation,' Marissa called over her shoulder as she went to her room. 'And don't sulk, Stevie.'

But Stevie did. She moped round the house doing odd bits of tidying up, tried to immerse herself in a thriller, but the same thoughts went round and round in her head. Yes, Marissa was right, she finally decided. She was 'in love', whatever that meant and for all the good it did her. She swore to herself and wished for the first time in her life that she didn't inhabit a woman's body, that she didn't have to repeat all the clichés. She tried to think sensibly about Jordan and finally sat down to write to him. He was too close to her for her to betray him dishonestly. She had better tell him that she was what Marissa called 'in love'.

Yet the words wouldn't come. All she could think of was James and the way she had scuttled childishly away from him. He probably didn't want her to come to Scotland with him anyway now, probably wouldn't approach her again at all. A pit formed at the base of her stomach and she crumpled up her writing paper and went to lie down on her bed. She hadn't the heart to write to Jordan properly. What could she tell him in any case—that she fancied herself in love with a man who was just having a little flirtation with her, a flirtation that was already over? She thought of Tara's overweening self-assurance, her mocking laughter. James was probably in bed with her again right now.

Stevie's heart began to race with a fury of misery. No, she would write to Jordan when she was calmer. She had to tell him, of course, but the whole thing would look different on another day, less significant. It would then be easier to explain.

The phone rang and Stevie got up from the bed.

James, she thought; it could only be James. Her heart
was in her mouth. But the voice at the other end of the
line was Tom Brewster's. He wanted to know whether
she was free to go to the theatre that evening. He would
be off in a few days and it would be nice to see her
again. Stevie was about to say no, when she thought
better of it. There was little point in lying around
agonising helplessly and the theatre was always a treat.
As it was, the evening passed pleasantly enough. She
didn't have to speak much and she was able to fend off
Tom's advances with a promise of seeing him next time
he was in London.

It's only with Genghis Khan that it doesn't work, a
little voice reminded her bitterly. Yes, she must be in
love, she thought dismally, feeling all the joy of life
drain out of her.

Late on Tuesday morning, Stevie was surprised to hear
on the internal line that Mr Brewster wanted a few
words with her. She walked nervously into his office,
wondering whether she had slipped up on anything. But
Mr Brewster greeted her with his usual good cheer.

'Sit down, Stevie, sit down.' He looked at her with
avuncular warmth as she crossed one slim leg over
another. 'I've never properly congratulated you on how
well you've been handling Reid. It seems he's pleased as
well.'

Stevie almost choked over her mumbled thank you.

'He rang me this morning to ask me whether we
could release you for a week or so, so that you could
accompany him on the Scottish assignment. It seems his
assistant is unavailable.'

Stevie felt her heart beginning to pound uncontrollably, her tongue growing thick in her mouth.

'Well, do you want to go, Stevie?' Mr Brewster
waited for her to speak.

'If it's all right with you,' she replied after what
seemed to her an unaccountably long time.

'Yes, of course, as long as you clear up any loose ends before you go, and brief Anthony on anything that needs following through. You haven't had a break since you've been with us, and by now you must be ready for one,' Mr Brewster smiled at her. When she didn't say anything, he continued, 'Reid says he'd like to leave a few days early. He wants to stop off and visit his family. But you can fix up the details with him directly.'

Stevie barely managed a few coherent sentences before escaping from Mr Brewster's office. Her mind was whirling. So James did still want her to go up to Scotland with him, despite the way they had parted. Her heart raced and she fought to still it. She must stay sensible. Of course, it was work and he needed an assistant. But why then invite her to come with him early?

'You look as if you've just been awarded some grand prize,' Anthony commented as she sat down at her desk.

'I'm going to Scotland to act as James Reid's assistant,' Stevie all but sang.

Anthony whistled, 'That's wonderful! It'll be an invaluable experience, much as I worry about your personal welfare among the ladykillers,' he added wryly.

'Yes, it *will* be instructive,' said Stevie, suddenly realising the truth of his words. 'And don't worry, Anthony, there's safety in numbers.' With all those models available, James wouldn't have a glance left for her, Stevie reflected with a sinking feeling. Never mind, she steadied herself. Anything was better than sitting round moping as she had been doing these last days.

James rang that afternoon, his voice casually polite. He'd been busy, he explained, doing an overdue Scandinavian assignment with Irena. Could she see the prints? Stevie asked. Yes, if she liked. He would have them dropped round that afternoon, and pick her up at the flat on Thursday morning. 'Bring some thick jumpers,' he added. 'The weather may not prove as balmy as London.'

At no point did he question that she might have decided not to go or say anything which might be construed as personal, Stevie noted. She steeled herself to follow his cue. Casual professionalism.

Just as she was about to leave the office that afternoon, a package arrived for her, and she opened it to find James's prints. They were good, she thought as she looked through them: Irena in swimming gear, playfully digging sandcastles; Irena in a boyish striped sweater naughtily tangled in a sail; Irena floating elegantly in evening dress past the admiring eyes of fishermen. With a pang of jealousy, Stevie passed the photographs over to Anthony. Yes, she would learn a lot from James Reid, as long as she could concentrate her mind on photography.

On the dot of ten on Thursday morning, Stevie heard the doorbell ring. She had been ready for what seemed an eternity and now she bolted for the door as if a starting gun had gone off. She opened it and stood there breathlessly as she looked at James, took in the steely grey-blue of his eyes, the high strong cheekbones, the straight nose and sensual mouth, the rugged maleness of him. She had forgotten the sheer magnetic power of his presence. It took her voice away.

'Hello, Stevie,' he drawled, his eyes mocking her evident discomfort. 'Would you like to invite me in for coffee before we set off?'

She nodded and managed to bring out a terse 'black or white?' as she guided him towards the kitchen.

'Do you live here alone?' He looked round the flat approvingly.

'With my sister—didn't I mention it?' She poured him a cup of coffee.

He shook his head. 'It's a nice place.'

He lowered his lithe form on to the sofa and

stretched his long legs lazily in front of him. Stevie suddenly realised that now the flat would constantly be filled with his presence. She shuddered.

James looked at her curiously. 'Come and sit down, Stevie,' he beckoned her towards him. 'I want to have a word with you before we leave.'

She walked towards him, acutely aware of his eyes on her, drawn as if by a hypnotist. She sat down as far away as she could without seeming rude.

He chuckled. 'You look like a tremulous deer facing a hunter!'

She didn't like the analogy and she made an effort to compose herself. It was a cool though bright morning and she had put on a pair of jeans tucked into high boots and a brick-red cotton knit jumper that brought out the sheen of her hair. Now she pulled her boots up higher with a slightly provocative gesture and leaned back into the sofa.

James was watching her and she thought she heard an impatient sigh escape his lips.

'Stevie,' he stretched out a hand to her, his face serious. She took it despite herself, wishing as soon as she felt the taut strength of his fingers closing over hers, that she hadn't. He stroked her fingers as he spoke and she knew from the tingling of her body that if he kissed her now she would once again be powerless to resist. She pulled her hand away from him and he let it go with a shrug.

'What I want to say, Stevie, is simply this: If you don't want me to touch you, as you made so emphatically clear when you rushed away the other night, I won't. You're saving yourself for this man— fine. We'll be friends and workmates. Just don't shudder every time I come close to you or you'll drop all the cameras!' He was trying to bring a smile to her face and Stevie knew she should be pleased, relieved. But her heart sank. She wanted him to touch her now, touch her as he had that night.

Instead she said, 'Good, I've been worrying for days

over the cameras.' Her voice quavered oddly as she made the attempted joke and she pulled her eyes away from him.

James put his mug down. 'Shall we set off, then? Where are your bags?'

Stevie pointed to her small case.

'Is that all?' He looked at her in wonder.

It was her turn to laugh, and the sound suddenly released her. She was off on an adventure, whatever the difficulties, and there was nothing she enjoyed more. 'I like travelling light,' she said. 'You never know when you might have to dash off.'

James gave her a stern glance and then his face lightened goodhumouredly. 'And if you need some extra togs, you can always try to wheedle an advance on your salary out of this skinflint of a Scotsman.'

Stevie stiffened. 'I'm not working for you,' she emphasized, 'just helping out. I'd never have *you* as a boss. That single day in the studio when you thought I was one of your models was quite enough to last me a lifetime!' The words came out in a rush and James burst into laughter.

'That bad, was I?'

Stevie nodded.

'Right, we'll have to make it up in extravagant expenses.'

'Thought you were a skinflint,' Stevie teased as they made their way down the stairs.

'Watch the way you talk to your friends, Ms Henderson,' he barked, but his eyes, blue in the sunlight, were smiling.

Stevie relaxed into the soft leather of the low-slung Jaguar. The car purred like a well-fed cat at James's touch. 'We'll start off on the motorway and then make some detours when the countryside becomes more interesting,' he explained, as he swung skillfully through traffic.

'I love it all,' said Stevie, 'just driving on open roads, anywhere. It reminds me of the U.S. of A.'

He pushed a cassette into the car radio. 'Something else to remind you of home.'

Stevie heard the plaintively wry voice of Bessie Smith belting out her incomparable blues, which sang simultaneously of a weary world wisdom and a love of life. She snuggled further into her seat, and unusually took one of the cigarettes James offered, dreamily watching the smoke curl upwards. Secretly she surveyed him from the corner of her eyes, the strong hands on the wheel, the hard profile beneath the dark hair, and thought how madly lucky she was to be sitting here, driving along, listening to music with this altogether wonderful man.

James drove quickly, steadily, not talking much except to point out spots of interest. In the early afternoon he pulled off the motorway.

'I've packed a picnic lunch,' he announced, 'and since the weather's holding, do you mind just stopping in a field somewhere near here, rather than at a restaurant?'

'I can't think of anything nicer,' Stevie smiled her pleasure.

They made their way down a narrow B-road banked by thick hedges until James pulled into a dirt lane which showed a breathtaking vista of undulant hills broken by dense copses. He took a large checked blanket and a picnic hamper out of the boot, and having locked the car with its precious load of cameras, they meandered along a footpath until they came to a small slope at the bottom of which a stream burbled.

Stevie smiled gleefully, 'It's just like the storybooks!' Sheep dotted the hillside on the other side of the stream. The sun played in and out of frothy clouds, making the landscape into a painter's canvas and warming their faces.

James spread the blanket and brought out what to Stevie's growling stomach was a veritable feast: a fresh French loaf, cold chicken and ham, tomatoes, celery and a flask of strong coffee.

Stevie watched him with a mounting sense of rapture. He seemed so totally at home in the open air, moving with the easy grace, the rippling energy of a stallion. His dark hair ruffled by the breeze, his eyes crystal clear in the light, his face strong in its self-composure, he reminded her again of the first impression she had had of him.

She laughed and he looked up at her like a startled animal. 'I just remembered my first thoughts when I saw you.'

'And was that so very comical?' His eyes thrust into her like steel.

But she nodded, still laughing. 'I thought you looked like one of those Marlboro Country he-men, all brawn and dreamy eyes.'

'And nothing but the smoke of bonfires in my head? Does that complete the picture? A perfect fashion photograper!' She could hear the anger in his voice, but she couldn't stop herself giggling and nodding.

'And here we are in Marlboro country—English style, I admit, sheep instead of mustang—but man's territory nonetheless,' Stevie added. She sat down on the blanket, drawing her knees up to her and looked at the fields with their clumps of light and dark grass.

James handed her a plate heaped with food and said nothing. Stevie bit in ravenously, not noticing the spark which kindled his eyes. She ate her fill and then stretched out languorously on the blanket, watching the fast-moving shapes of the clouds.

James's voice startled her. 'And you, of course, are totally impervious to the attractions of "man's territory", as you call it?'

She looked at him from beneath thick lashes, her green eyes dreamy and slow to register his changed mood. There was an arrogant tilt to his jaw, an air of menace in his eyes. A little tremor made its way across her body and she closed her eyes to block out his face.

'Totally,' she said with emphasis, something daring her to meet his challenge.

'Well, we shall see about that, Ms Stevie Henderson.' His voice was icy. With a crushing force his lips were on hers, biting into her, claiming her mouth brutally. Stevie tried to push him away, hammering at his back with her fists, but her stomach turned liquid against the firmness of his body, and a rich warm tide swept through her, robbing her of resistance, making her cleave to him so that her lips opened in response to his and met their now gentler insistence. Suddenly he moved away from her and stood to his full height, looming over her prostrate body, blocking the sun from her view.

'Not so totally impervious, I would suggest,' he said laconically.

'Bastard!' Stevie brought it out before she could stop herself.

He laughed, a cold icy sound. 'If you don't want me to touch you, Stevie, then don't taunt me. We're not children,' he said dangerously. And then, as if he had had enough of her presence, he busied himself with clearing their picnic spot.

Stevie rose and with a semblance of helping him, took plates and cups down to the stream to wash. She wanted to create a distance between them. He was right, of course, she had taunted him, but that didn't give him the right to break their agreement. He had made his point. Any time he wanted to force her, she would succumb to him. It brought a bitter taste of humiliation to her mouth, and she walked back towards him feeling that all pleasure had gone from her day.

She could feel him watching her scale the incline, but she kept her eyes from his. When she reached him and finally met his gaze, she realised he was laughing at her. 'Don't sulk. I won't do it again ... unless ...' his eyes twinkled mischievously. He held out his hand and said in imitation of a Western drawl, 'Shake, pardner. This is Marlboro Country.'

His grin was irresistible, and Stevie took his hand briefly and tried a smile.

'And don't forget you're a beautiful woman,' he whispered in her ear, 'and I'm just a poor brainless he-man. So do watch the way you stretch out that long lovely body of yours. I'm not at work now.' The mockery in his tone was unbearable and she raised her hand to hit him, but he caught her arm midway.

'Bad move,' he suggested, 'unless you want more of the same.'

Stevie pulled away from him, running as fast as she could. She knew if she didn't she would burst into tears. But by the time she reached the car, he was right behind her. 'Better?' he asked calmly. 'Shall we go, then?'

She nodded, and they set off in the purring Jaguar. She was oblivious now to the changes in the country around them, but she looked straight ahead, as if her attention were rapt by some insurmountable power.

Suddenly James started to talk. 'Did I tell you we were stopping off to see my mother for a few days?'

Stevie was jolted into attention. 'Your mother?' she stammered. 'With me?' Her mouth dropped open as he nodded.

He smiled at her nervousness. 'You'll like her, she's a good lady, and I think she'll like you. Though she hasn't always taken kindly to my women.' He chuckled wryly as if he were remembering previous ordeals.

'Well, luckily I'm not one of your women,' said Stevie with a bitter emphasis.

He shot her a dark look and then continued, as if she hadn't said anything.

'She's rather seriously ill now, though she won't admit it. Carries on regardless.'

Stevie found herself growing interested. 'Does anyone look after her?'

'There's Beattie who helps out. She's been with the family for years. My father died over ten years ago,' James offered.

'And there are no brothers or sisters?'

He hesitated and Stevie saw an expression of naked pain pass over his face. Finally he answered, 'An older sister. She lives in Edinburgh with her husband and children. They visit as frequently as they can.'

'I see.' Stevie didn't want her curiosity to get the better of her and corner him into secretive silence, so despite the questions which leapt to her mind, she kept her tongue.

It had started to rain and the only sound in the car now was the rhythmic whoosh of the windscreen wipers. The sky had grown ominously dark and the countryside looked bleak, forbidding. James was driving more slowly than before over the winding roads, his eyes intently fixed in front of him. Stevie noticed that his face looked strained, that his broad shoulders were tensed. All at once she had an overwhelming urge to touch him, to soothe his evident fatigue. Without thinking, she stretched out an arm and began to rub the base of his neck with firm circular motions.

'Blissful,' he murmured, throwing her a questioning glance.

His warmth began to envelop her and Stevie drew her hand away.

'Thanks,' he said simply.

She shrugged, 'I thought you looked tired.'

'I didn't get enough sleep last night, I guess.'

Stevie suddenly had an image of him lying on a tumbled bed with Irena or Tara. 'Your harem keeping you busy?' The comment was out with a scathing bluntness, before she could stop it.

She was unprepared for his roar of laughter. 'Jealous, Stevie? I could include you. Just say the word.'

She flushed hotly and pulled as far towards the door as she could without falling out. 'Certainly not,' she managed as emphatically as she could. 'I like my men to myself.'

'Do you now? I'll have to make a note of that,' he

said ironically. After a moment, he added, his voice light, 'I was working, Stevie, on the book, that one you've taken against so.'

Dismally aware of her own folly, Stevie was silent. At last she asked shyly, 'What is it about?'

'Are you really interested?' He sounded surprised.

'Of course I am.'

She could see his firm mouth turning up in a smile.

'I'll tell you over dinner, then. There's a rather fine hotel not too far from here and we could use a break.'

CHAPTER SIX

JAMES swung the car into a tree-lined drive which gave way after a few hundred yards to a gabled stone structure. The warm glow of lights from its windows looked strangely out of place in this remote rainswept landscape which seemed foreign both to electricity and life. Stevie had spent the last few miles eagerly peering through heavy rain and darkness for some sign of habitation, until her eyes had grown weary with the strain.

She was surprised to find that her watch showed only eight o'clock.

'Tired?' James queried.

Stevie shook her head. 'Just need to stretch.'

He drove the car to what seemed to be the back of the hotel. The car park was almost full and Stevie wondered vaguely where all these people had suddenly come from. They had met hardly a dozen pairs of headlights in the last while.

James dug out a mac from somewhere in the boot and held it over both of them as they ran through the driving rain towards the hotel entrance. 'Phew!' Stevie exclaimed as they reached the interior. 'If this weather doesn't break, you're not going to get many pictures taken.'

'We'll just have to start at the crack of dawn. It's often clear then.' James smiled mysteriously. 'Or you'll simply have to assist me for weeks!'

A small pulse began to beat at the base of Stevie's stomach and she looked up to see whether he was joking. But she couldn't read his expression. 'I'd better freshen up a little,' she said, suddenly aware of the faces around them, her damp hair and rumpled sweater.

James pointed her towards a women's room and she made her way gratefully towards it.

The damp had made her hair curl wildly round her face, giving her the air of some woodland creature. She grimaced, rubbed her face and as much as she could of her hair dry with a towel, and applied a little blusher to her paleness. But, unhappy with the effect, she washed it off. James had the distinct ability to make her feel dissatisfied with an appearance she didn't otherwise much notice. Either she felt herself to be too attractive—which she remembered he had said he didn't altogether approve of, though she wondered if that had to do solely with the work context—or she felt dismally unattractive. She shrugged, smoothed her jeans over her legs, passed a brush as best she could through the thick mass of her hair and strolled out to the lobby. She wouldn't let him distress her, she promised herself, but as soon as she felt his eyes on her, surveying her slowly, her skin started to burn.

'If I didn't know better, I'd say you'd turned into one of those Pre-Raphaelite maidens, all brooding sensuality under not-too-steady control.'

'Luckily you know better!' She shot him a deadly glance which brought laughter to his eyes. Casually he put an arm around her waist and led her towards the restaurant, a sprawling room warmed by a blazing open fire.

'The food is simple but good,' James offered, while a plump young waitress handed them their menus. The girl cast shy doe eyes at James, who engaged her in conversation.

Another conquest! Stevie fumed silently.

'I've seen that girl grow up over the years,' said James as if he had read her thoughts. 'I stop here regularly when I'm passing through.'

Stevie coloured and turned her attention to the plate of smoked salmon which the girl had placed in front of her.

'Tell me about this book, then,' she said after she had swallowed a few delicious mouthfuls and her face had cooled.

James looked at her reflectively as if he were considering the scope of her understanding.

She bridled. 'I'm not totally devoid of intelligence, you know!'

He laughed, 'Did I suggest you were? The book, as you might have guessed, is about photography. But the approach is, I think, a little unusual. It's not a "how to" book, more of a personal memoir combined with an attempt to understand what role photographs play in our lives.'

He warmed to his subject as Stevie began to ask questions. She soon became aware of the fine edge of his intellect, as well as something else—an acute moral sense. As he talked it became clear to her that he had given up news photography because he had begun to see it as exploitative, a totally sensationalist invasion of other people's lives. He told her of an incident in Ethiopia. He had found himself photographing a dying woman and her starving child and suddenly in a flash, the whole absurdity of the affair came home to him. Rather than going to help her, fetching medicine or food, he had taken photograph after photograph out of simple routine compulsion, as if the human life, the suffering in front of him were simply an object for him to turn into news. It was then that he had realised that he couldn't carry on with the work much longer.

'But if you, people like you, didn't take those photographs of misery as well as everything else, how are the rest of us to know what's going on? And if we don't know, we can't help to change things,' Stevie intervened.

'That's true enough, Stevie. But on the whole we've become so inured to images of horror that we have little capacity left to take the misery in,' he frowned. 'In any case, the way these photographs are presented to us in

the press, they become random moments, totally
divorced from their subjects' lives. It neutralises the
horror, because these people never step off the page as
people with distinct individual lives, a past and a
present.'

Stevie suddenly remembered the photographs
Anthony had shown her that James had taken in the
Middle East. 'Your photographs weren't always like
that,' she said.

A light flickered in his eyes. 'I didn't know anyone
had noticed.' He raised his glass to her and smiled.

But she was too engrossed in the subject to be
deflected. 'And is that why you gave it all up?'

A shadow passed over his strong face. 'Partly,' he
mumured. 'I turned my camera to neutral objects for a
while—industrial equipment, oil rigs, and then other
things came up.' He deliberately changed the subject,
telling her about the region they were in, about the
foothills of the Highlands he came from.

Stevie listened with only half an ear, eating her steak
slowly and pondering over what he had said. He was,
she decided as objectively as she could, a singularly
extraordinary man. She looked up at him now with
something akin to awe in her face. 'And you'll never go
back to doing that kind of work now?'

'Perhaps, in different circumstances. We'll see what
the future brings. Meanwhile I'm beginning to enjoy
this short excursion into glamour,' he chuckled wryly.
'But you look sleepy. We'd better head off again and
you can snooze in the car. I told Mother we'd probably
arrive in the small hours.'

When they stepped outside, the rain was beating
down with torrential insistence. James groaned, 'This is
hopeless! We won't make any headway. We might as
well spend the night here and get an early start.'

Stevie nodded in relief. She couldn't imagine James
seeing more than two feet ahead in the downpour. And
the roads would be dangerously wet.

'Wait here and I'll get our bags.' He dashed out into the rain and was back minutes later, water streaming down his handsome face. 'I'm glad you travel light,' he smiled at her, 'or I'd be a drowned man!'

Stevie waited while he took care of the reception formalities and then agreed to his invitation to have a drink.

'Now that I'm not driving, a stiff brandy would do wonders for the soul,' he chuckled as he led her into a comfortable, firelit bar, crowded with people. 'What about you?'

'Yes, why not?' Stevie acquiesced. 'This is, in part, a holiday, after all.' She looked up at him, her mouth and eyes curling in a smile.

James eyed her strangely. She had no idea how ravishing she looked with the glow of the fire burnishing the gold of her hair and casting playful lights into her wide green eyes. 'Is there something wrong?' she asked, taking in his look.

He passed her a brandy glass and gave her a slow, languid wink as he eased his supple length on to a low chair. Then he cleared his throat. 'It's rather crowded here tonight, Stevie, and I'm afraid they only had one room left.'

She stiffened, a frightened look coming into her eye. 'But that's impossible!' she breathed.

A flash of anger darkened his face. 'Don't you trust me?'

She didn't dare meet his gaze. How could she tell him that it was herself she didn't trust, her own traitorous body?

'There are twin beds, so you have nothing to worry about. And I'm not so desperately in need of female company that I have to force myself on you,' he said derisively.

Stevie winced at his tone. In one blazing gulp she downed her brandy. The liquid burned her throat, making her cough.

James shook his head. 'And they told me these American women had a sense of adventure!'

'There are other kinds of adventure than those which lead one to the bedroom,' Stevie retorted, holding her head high.

'You don't say!' The mockery in his tone enraged her, but she could think of nothing to counter it with, so she sat there stiffly, avoiding his eyes.

'Shall we go up, then?' he queried casually, when he had finished his brandy.

Stevie stumbled to her feet, still fighting shy of his eyes. She followed him up a wide staircase and along a corridor to a door with the number 27 engraved on it in bronze. The number seemed to burn into her mind with a painful slowness.

James turned the key and switched on a light. Stevie's eyes fled to the room's centre where she saw two beds made up separately, but so close to one another they were touching.

'We can move them to opposite sides of the room,' said James, catching the direction of her glance. His tone chaffed her.

'That won't be necessary,' she flung back at him.

'Oh?' He looked at her ironically, his blue eyes playful. 'I'll leave you to it, then. Don't wait up for me.' He closed the door behind him and Stevie found herself alone in the room.

Feeling like a fool, she picked up her bag which had been neatly placed on a case rack, and rifled through it, pulling out her long nightie. Then, with an air of defiance, she undressed and made for the bathroom. The thought of a shower was irresistible, and tying her hair back, she let the warm spiky water beat down on her and drive away her jumbled thoughts. Having wiped herself dry with a large fluffy towel, she pulled on her nightie, switched on a small lamp and climbed into the bed. But sleep wouldn't come. She lay there rigid waiting for James to return.

An interminable length of time seemed to have passed before she heard the door opening softly. She squeezed her eyes tightly shut, pretending sleep, but she could make out the sound of each of James's movements as he crossed the room, unzipped his case, made for the bathroom and then emerged again. Through lowered lids, Stevie hazarded a look. He was standing with his back to her, wearing nothing but a pair of briefs. Her eyes roved over his muscled back, his trim hips and powerful legs. She caught her breath as a wave of sensation spread from the pit of her stomach over the whole of her body, enclosing her in a dizzy longing. Suddenly he turned. She screwed her eyes shut.

A low chuckle escaped his lips. Then the light went out and the bed beside her creaked a little. A pair of firm lips brushed her forehead. 'Goodnight, Stevie,' James whispered.

She woke to find a single ray of sunlight peeking through a parting in the curtains. As her thoughts focussed, she glanced quickly round the room, but there was no sign of James. Disappointment coursed through her. She reached for her watch, which registered seven o'clock. She stretched lazily. She didn't feel like getting up yet, so she closed her eyes again, reaching a hand over to feel the indentation of James's head on his pillow. The sensation filled her with a mellow warmth that lulled her back to sleep.

When she next opened her eyes, he was sitting next to her, watching her, an indolent smile playing over his face. Unconsciously she returned his look, her eyes catching fire from his.

'The Sleeping Beauty awakes,' he said in a soft voice.

'Stevie's hair tumbled over her shoulders as she sat up. 'Am I very late?' she asked lazily.

He shook his head. 'I've had some tea brought up and when you've finished that we can go down for breakfast.' He passed her a cup and as he moved close, she breathed in the tangy smell of fern, a crisp outdoor scent.

'You've been walking?' she questioned suspiciously. 'You should have woken me. I'd love a walk.'

'After breakfast,' he consoled her. 'And bring a bathing suit. It may just be warm enough for a swim.'

Stevie's eyes sparkled. 'A real holiday,' she said shyly, and took a sip of the hot strong tea.

'A real holiday,' James confirmed. 'It's going to be a beautiful day and I've rung to say we'd be late. I'll meet you downstairs when you're ready.' He left her drinking her tea.

A smile played round Stevie's lips and she jumped out of bed, quickly pulled on a red and white striped bikini, her jeans and a red shirt with a wide midi collar. Throwing the curtains back, she saw sunlight playing through morning mist and illuminating a lushly green valley. Suddenly she felt exhilarated, and as she brushed some order into her hair, she vowed that she wouldn't spoil this beautiful day by behaving like a silly child. A sudden guilty thought of Jordan came to her mind and she pushed it ruthlessly away.

Following the smell of bacon and fragrant coffee, she made her way downstairs.

James was munching some toast and reading a newspaper. She slipped into the chair beside him, 'Where's this food, then? I'm starving again!' Stevie looked waggishly at the man at her side.

He caught her mood. 'Your every wish, my dear young lady,' and before his sentence was out, the waitress had deposited two plates before them. Stevie dug into the bacon and eggs with relish, wiping her plate clean with thick chunks of buttered toast.

James watched her with amusement. 'In good spirits this morning?'

'Irrepressible, so don't try to repress them,' Stevie added in mock warning.

'Me?' A look of exaggerated innocence moulded

his features comically.

She laughed and gulped down some hot coffee. 'I'm ready when you are.'

'At your service, Ms Henderson.' He pulled his chair back, picked up a towel she hadn't noticed and bowed lightheartedly.

Stevie all but bounced out of the hotel and, then trying to match her strides to his, walked with him briskly in the direction of the valley. The air had a balmy hush to it, a moist morning fragrance which seemed too fragile to contain words. Perky little spring flowers poked their heads through the dewy grass. Stevie suddenly felt as if she'd never been happier. With a burst of energy, she started to run down the slope. Letting gravity carry her ever more quickly, she veered precariously round spiky bursts of heather, leapt lightly over stones, like a gambolling lamb friskily exploring new ground.

'Stop there, lassie!' James caught up with her and put a staying arm round her waist. 'We're going in that direction.' He pointed to the left. She looked up into his strong laughing face, the crystal clarity of his eyes in the open air, and felt as if the earth were suddenly swirling dizzily round her. She flashed James a smile and raced away in the direction he had pointed.

Within minutes, she found herself by a stream, perhaps even a small river, she thought as she noted the speed with which the water was travelling over the rocks near its bank. The sun glistened merrily over its surface. With the sureness of an experienced river swimmer, Stevie knew at a moment's glance exactly where the water grew deep and then shallow again for no explicable reason. She stripped off her jeans and shirt, gasped as she felt the water's coldness and then, without allowing herself to hesitate, walked clear of the rocks and dived in. An audible gasp escaped her as she rose to the surface.

'Cold enough for a North American?' James was

right beside her, though she hadn't until this moment been aware of his closeness.

'Icy!' Stevie gasped again, feeling that the water would freeze her into position if she didn't lunge out.

James matched his strokes to hers and they swam until she felt her teeth beginning to chatter. He ordered her out. 'We're getting a little too close to the falls,' he explained.

As she stumbled over the sharp rocks, he put out a hand to her and pulled her out. She was shivering, despite the sun which had now grown a little warmer.

'A run back to our clothes to get the blood circulating again?' queried James, his eyes flickering briefly over her shapely form.

She nodded, afraid to speak through her chattering teeth or to look at him directly.

'Watch the stones,' he cautioned, as she headed off. He kept pace with her, making sure she didn't stumble, running supply by her side. Stevie could feel the warmth just beginning to return to her limbs when she spied their starting point. Panting, she flopped down on the spiky grass, cradling her face in her arms. Suddenly she felt James rubbing her dry with the thick towel, urging her limbs into life. She turned on her back, and the sight of him kneeling above her took her breath away. The broad expanse of his chest above the taut waist, the straight column of his neck, the strong, rugged planes of his face. Without knowing what possessed her, she stretched out an arm to touch him, letting it trail up his muscled shoulders to the moist hair at the back of his neck.

'Stevie!' Her name was hoarse on his lips as he brought them down to meet hers with an urgent sweetness. Their warmth suffused her and she opened her mouth to him, letting her growing yearning find solace in his arms. Cradling her head, he clasped her to him and moulded her body to his own hardness, suffusing her face, her neck, her swelling breasts with moistly tender kisses. With a need of their own, Stevie's fingers explored his skin, seeking out unknown regions, drawing out low moans from him that kindled her senses into a new desperate sensitivity. She felt a mute stirring, a blissful awakening deep inside her, and when their lips met again, it was with a passion that shook them both; a man and a woman clinging together in a fiercely shared need.

James murmured her name again. She heard it as from a great distance and opened her eyes wide to him. He stroked her hair. 'Stevie, I can't make love to you here,' he said gently. 'Much as I want to. Can you hear the children?'

It was as if she had been jolted into consciousness. She rolled away from him. A low painful laugh rose to her lips. 'Saved by the bell once again,' she said, turning to look at him. The sheer beauty of his face as he gazed at her gravely, staggered her.

'There won't be any warning bells tonight,' he said seriously.

'Yes, but by then I hope to have found my more common senses,' she returned, equally serious. She reached for her jeans and tugged them on with difficulty over her still wet bathing suit, standing to wriggle them over her hips.

James pulled her down on to the grass beside him and looked at her forbiddingly. 'Stevie, no games, now. You want me as much as I want you.'

She shrugged, meeting his eyes bravely. 'We can't always have what we want,' she said, her voice clear.

'Why not?' Anger darkened his features. 'Because of your man back home, a man who doesn't care enough for you to keep you by his side, a man who lets you run off and . . .' his derisive gesture was self-explanatory.

'There are other things in life than *that*,' she repeated his gesture tersely. And then suddenly, uncontrollably, she felt the tears beginning to trickle down her face and mount into sobs. She got up and ran from him, wanting to find a dark corner in which to hide. It wasn't Jordan she was worrying about, she wanted to tell him. It was James, James who carried her into areas of feeling she had never before travelled, who swept all reason away as soon as he looked at her; and who would leave her trembling out in the cold, like Irena, as soon as he had had his fill of her. I love you, she wanted to shout. But it was a wasted emotion, unless he returned it, unless it somehow became the centre of a shared life.

He had come up quietly behind her and now he draped an arm loosely over her shoulders. 'Here, put this on,' he said gently handing her her blouse. She looked at him through tear-filled eyes. 'It's all right Stevie. I won't push you into anything. It's not my style. Stop worrying.' He smiled at her, though his eyes were sombre. 'I keep forgetting that years aside, I'm an eternity older than you.' He chucked her whimsically under the chin.

'I'm not a child,' Stevie said defensively.

'No,' his glance raked over her body suggestively, 'I've noticed that.'

She lowered her eyes. He was still in his bathing briefs and suddenly she noticed a deep scar on the side of his thigh.

'What's that?' she asked, drawn to finger it.

He flinched away and then laughed bitterly. 'That,' he said, 'is a souvenir of my stupidity.'

She looked up at him, not understanding.

'A little left-over from my days of heroism on the battlefronts of the world. You shoot people,' he clicked an imaginary camera, 'and quite naturally, they shoot back. It's a spontaneous impulse.'

Stevie felt her knees grow weak. 'You sound very bitter about it,' she said in a hushed voice.

He shrugged his shoulders and walked towards his clothes. Pulling them on, he looked at her evenly. 'I'm not really, any more. It was just a particularly stupid, an unnecessary incident—in the Middle East. And the man I was with, a journalist and a good friend, is dead to prove it. I was lucky.' The deadly irony in his voice made her think that he would have preferred to be the one to die.

Meeting the pained look in her eyes, he put out a finger to stroke her cheek tenderly. 'It's over with. Forget it now.'

They climbed up the hill together, coming across the children whose voices James had heard.

'My bell,' Stevie laughed in self-mockery.

He shot her a questioning glance, then bent to pick up a football which had rolled in front of them. He threw it back with steady precision, so that it landed directly in the small boy's arms. He laughed, 'I've missed my calling!' He waved to the boys, his face suddenly happy.

'Do you like children?' Stevie asked, wondering at herself as soon as she had said it.

He nodded. 'It's probably time I had some.' He threw her another quizzical glance.

She swallowed a hard lump which had risen to her throat.

'And you?' he returned her question.

'Oh yes,' Stevie managed blithely. 'When I grow up I shall have four, and we'll live in the country and go swimming all summer and skiing all winter and read books in between.'

'And your man back home is going to support this blissful idyll, I expect.' James's voice was heavy with irony.

'With my help, of course. I couldn't give up working for ever,' she said, misinterpreting his intent.

They walked the rest of the way to the hotel in silence. It was only when they were well under way, travelling smoothly through the increasingly beautiful countryside which now and then gave way to breathtaking vistas of the sea, that James spoke again.

'Stevie, I want to ask something of you.'

She looked up at him expectantly.

He pulled into a layby and turned to her, his eyes clear in his rugged face. Once again Stevie was seized by the desire to touch him, but she kept her hands tightly clenched. He gazed at her thoughtfully for a moment and then began to speak. 'It's an odd favour, but I hope you'll grant it nonetheless.' He paused as if searching for the right words.

'My mother, as I told you, is very ill. I don't think she'll live for very long now, and there's one thing that she wants desperately: to see me settled down.' He laughed. As if the idea were an extraordinary one, Stevie thought.

'I thought you might—no, rather we might, pretend to her that we were engaged.'

'What!' Stevie gasped, totally unprepared for his words.

'Well, if you think it would be that terrifying, we'll forget it.' He moved to start the engine and then thought better of it. 'It wouldn't be that difficult, Stevie.' He turned to her again and took her hand. 'We do rather like each other.' His eyes grazed over her provocatively and Stevie felt an answering flame leaping up inside her.

'But why me?' a strangled voice emerged through her lips.

He shrugged. 'She'll take to you. She doesn't usually much like my women.'

Stevie swallowed hard. At last she said, 'Very well, I'll pretend to be your—woman.' She brought out the last word disparagingly.

He laughed, a pure joyous laugh. 'My *wife*, my wife-to-be, Stevie. Let's seal it with a kiss.' He reached over to draw her to him and claim her lips, but she turned her face away.

'Not until I have my ring,' she said mischievously.

'That can be easily arranged. All it requires is a little

detour.' He started the car with a roar and whizzed it with new alacrity along the narrow road.

Stevie was suddenly filled with trepidation. She didn't really want to take the charade that far. She could manage to be warmly polite to James's mother for a few days, but to acquire a ring and then wear it like a strange weight around her finger, constantly reminding her of a game that she wished were real—yes, she wished it, she admitted to herself bluntly—that would be too much.

'I was only teasing, James,' she said quietly. 'I don't really want a ring.'

'Oh yes, you do,' his voice was firm. 'It will be the crowning touch to convince Mother.'

He popped a cassette into the radio and the jubilant chords of the Emperor Concerto filled the car with sound.

Stevie was amazed both by the liveliness and stately elegance of Edinburgh with its fine Georgian squares and wonderfully symmetrical grey stone façades. It had the unexpected grandeur of an old European capital.

James laughed at her enthusiasm. 'You thought we only produced football hooligans and wee drams, did you?'

'And Robert Burns and fashion photographers,' Stevie responded to his good humour.

'We can forget about the last for a while,' he said with mock severity, and pulled the car to a halt. They were now in the old town, guarded by the mighty rock of Edinburgh Castle, and they ambled cheerfully along a winding cobbled street, its upper level graced by carefully restored tenements, and past the intimate yet stately elegance of parliament houses.

'Here, this is where we want to go.' James took her hand and guided her towards a small shop. Stevie looked into a window which displayed carefully crafted jewellery, old and new: beautifully wrought gold and silver set with stones that caught the limpid sun and warmed it in their depths.

'This is ridiculous,' she said in a disgruntled tone.

James all but dragged her into the shop and when she refused to put her mind to choosing what she liked, he had the assistant bring out tray after tray of rings, from which he carefully selected a few for her to try.

Stevie noticed that these were all set with jade or emeralds.

'To match your eyes,' he explained, and waved away her protests about the price. 'I may be a parsimonious Scot,' he grinned, 'but when it comes to serious matters like engagement rings, a bit of Woolworth's tin would never do.'

After a little persuasion Stevie began to try on the rings. One in particular caught her fancy: a simple twisted old gold band with an oval-shaped emerald stone, the colour of darkly lush valley grass after a heavy rain. But she refused to choose between the rings, despite James's urging that she must suit herself.

'No,' she protested, 'it's *your* ring.'

Anger darkened his eyes, 'That one, then.' He brusquely picked up the ring Stevie had favoured and after a moment's hesitation, slipped it slowly on to her third finger. Their eyes met and Stevie read a brooding intensity in his that startled her. She lowered her eyes and said quietly, 'It's the one I preferred, too.'

They were both suddenly aware of the shop assistant eyeing them curiously. With an abrupt gesture, James drew Stevie into his arms and hugging her tightly placed a mellow kiss on her lips. 'Just practising,' he whispered as she stiffened. He winked at her wickedly and then turned to the girl who was gazing up at him with admiring eyes.

Stevie's heart sank as she realised what the ring cost, and its weight oppressed her, a constant reminder of the charade in which she was engaged.

But James seemed decidedly cheerful, and as they left

the shop and strolled down the narrow street, he put his arm round her shoulders. 'Rehearsing,' he insisted again as she tried to draw away. 'The curtain goes up very soon.' He kept his arm firmly round her, while Stevie tried desperately to steel herself against the effects of his touch.

When they were back in the car he turned to her, his jaw tensed. 'Stevie, please try to act as if you enjoy my company. Look,' he said to her sounding, she thought, like a director prompting a recalcitrant actress, 'we're happy, you're engaged to the most wonderful man in the world—from my mother's point of view,' he chuckled at her response to his arrogance, 'and I'm wildly, passionately in love with a rather headstrong, somewhat recalcitrant, devastatingly attractive New England *Ms*.'

A contradictory mixture of emotions choked Stevie's response to this list of coolly delivered propositions. But when his lips pressed hers in a kiss which was real enough to send the blood clamouring through her veins, she suddenly knew what she must do if she were to survive this weekend of theatre.

'I think the scenario is clear,' she said innocently when she regained her breath. She smoothed her shirt, just a little suggestively, over the curve of her breasts, straightened her jeans with slightly provocative movements, and then, when he had started the car, eased closer to him, placing her hand casually on the base of his strong neck where the dark hair curled.

He looked at her questioningly, and Stevie smiled in sweet innocence, her green eyes wide in her face. 'I'm using my last few minutes of rehearsal time,' she explained, letting her fingers play through his hair.

James laughed, a short, sharp laugh. 'Just don't overdo it, Stevie, or you never know what may happen.'

She pretended she hadn't heard the threat in his voice, and for the rest of the way she stayed as close to him as she dared, steeling her body not to respond to the sensations she herself was precipitating.

The countryside had turned softly green now and as they drove on twisting roads, she was occasionally reminded of the wooded hills, valleys and streams of New England. She laughed at the assortment of strange names the road signs announced, and James explained that many of them simply referred to no more than houses and their outlying farms,

'In my grandfather's time, half of them belonged to members of the family. Enormous houses, castles some of them, too big by half for anyone to run now, except rock stars and rich Americans looking for ancestral roots. They live there for a while, grow bored, then leave. The places get run down.' He shook his head with a mixture of sadness and disdain.

Then Stevie saw his face brighten. 'We're here.' He pulled on to a well-beaten dirt track which led over a small bridge and through rolling fields. Stevie saw cattle, then grain, then a heather-topped hill and finally a small stone cottage. 'Hold on just a moment,' he said as he got out of the car. She watched him walk towards the house, his long legs carrying him with athletic vigour. Her pulse began to flutter and she forced herself to sit calmly. She saw James coming out of the house with a buxom round-faced woman, her dress covered by a large apron. Wiping her perspiring hands on her jeans, Stevie prepared to greet James's mother.

'This is Catherine,' said James, as Stevie stepped out of the car. Stevie was a little taken aback at the woman's youthful air, not at all an aspect she had expected. Nonetheless, she hid her surprise and greeted James's mother politely. 'I'm so pleased to meet you, Mrs Reid.'

The woman stepped back, looking at James inquiringly and when he burst out laughing, she said, 'Och, lass, I'm not Mrs Reid, I'm Catherine Buchanan.'

Stevie flushed, apologising. 'Catherine and her

husband look after the farm,' James explained. 'We'll be at the house in a few minutes.' He got back into the car and Stevie followed, feeling decidedly silly.

'You should have warned me,' she murmured.

'I didn't think,' he apologised. 'It's all so familiar to me.'

Now the road opened up into a wider paved drive and Stevie's mouth fell open. 'Is this it?' she asked, her voice tremulous.

In front of them was an impressive white stucco structure made up of a hodge-podge of styles—comfortable manor house in front, tiny castle complete with turret at the back, clematis-covered stables at the side—all with an eccentricity of detail that sent her eyes reeling from point to point.

James laughed at her expression. 'Perhaps I should have prepared you better. But I promise you we're not quite so mad as Carn Liath suggests. It's just that my grandfather had a sense of architectural humour.' He switched off the car's engine. 'Ready, Stevie?' He squeezed her hand briefly.

She met his eyes for a lingering moment and then smiled up at him boldly. 'As ready as I'll ever be!'

CHAPTER SEVEN

BEFORE James and Stevie had reached the front door, a tall handsome woman opened it. Steel-grey hair pulled back into a tidy bun, she was leaning heavily on a cane, but she moved towards them with a proud erectness, her shoulders and head thrown back in welcoming anticipation. James embraced her, almost lifting her off her feet, while Stevie stood shyly to one side. As the woman edged back to laugh protestingly at James's assault, Stevie was aware of their resemblance, the same strong face and clarity of eye.

Still laughing, she turned her gaze on Stevie. 'And this must be Stevie Henderson.' She examined Stevie's face shrewdly and then stretched out her arm in warm welcome. 'I'm very, very pleased, my dear, enormously pleased.'

As Stevie took her hand timidly, Mrs Reid's eyes twinkled. 'Don't worry, my dear, if James has opted for you, you won't have to leap any hurdles for me. I should think you have your work cut out for you already!' She looked at James teasingly.

'Now don't frighten Stevie, Mother.'

As they turned to go into the house, Stevie threw James a dark glance. When had he managed to convey to his mother that he and Stevie were engaged, if he had only asked her to play the role of fiancée that very morning? Or had she misinterpreted the sense of Mrs Reid's words?

Whatever the case, James seemed totally untroubled. He placed an arm casually round Stevie's shoulder and by the time they were ushered into a drawing room whose two large corner windows opened on to a breathtaking expanse of rolling hills, Stevie was so

121

transfixed by what was in front of her that her natural enthusiasm took over from any more worrying emotions.

'Why, this is wonderful!' she exclaimed, excitement making her voice shrill. 'Simply wonderful! I couldn't see any of this from the road.'

Mother and son laughed together. 'Yes, we like it too,' Mrs Reid said, 'especially when the weather is as good as it is today. But do sit down, you two, while I get some drinks. Beattie is just preparing some cold lunch and we can eat in a moment.'

'I'll get the drinks, Mother. You sit.'

Having filled her eyes with the wonders of the landscape, Stevie now looked round the room they were sitting in. It was large, but not as enormous as the exterior of the house had led her to expect, but again it contained this strangely exciting mixture of elements. The corner windows opposite the ones which opened to the landscape, were made out of coloured glass and formed a small alcove, a step up from the rest of the room. The glass cast oddly playful shapes of tinted light on the highly polished floor. There was little clutter, a few well-chosen pieces of furniture arranged to break up the room into separate intimate parts, a large oak fireplace surrounded by old tiles, flower-covered sofas and chairs, small side tables. The whole gave off an air of gracious comfort.

Mrs Reid watched Stevie surveying the room. 'I always forget what an odd place this must seem until we have a new visitor,' she said.

'It's a glorious room,' Stevie replied, then giggled. 'I thought you lived in the cottage up the road, and I called Catherine Mrs Reid!'

The laugh lines on the older woman's face etched her smile. 'James *is* naughty,' she said just as her son appeared with a bottle of sherry and another of white wine.

'Stop talking behind my back, Mother,' he teased. 'I

didn't want Stevie to love me for your delightful front
room.'

Stevie let her eyes travel lazily over his face as he
handed her a glass of wine. With the grace of a natural
actor, he bent to graze her lips with a light kiss.

'Now what's this?' a loud stern voice called from the
doorway 'The lad's being frivolous again!'

Stevie looked up to identify the owner of the broad
rolling 'r's'.

'Beattie!' James lifted the small stout woman off the
floor and whirled her round.

'Aye, Beattie it is. And I'm glad to see you're not in a
foul temper today, lad, as you were the last time I saw
you.'

'Sh, Beattie!' James kissed the woman's vividly pink
cheeks and ushered her towards Stevie. 'This, Stevie, is
the redoubtable Beattie, and if you misbehave even for
an instant, she'll wallop you with one of those rolling
pins she keeps especially for the purpose!'

'He's got a powerful imagination, the lad has.'
Beattie shook Stevie's proffered hand. 'But don't you
listen to him. I used my hands and no rolling pins!' She
threw James a ferocious glance.

'Beattie has, as the saying goes, brought me up by
hand,' James explained smilingly to Stevie.

'And a hard job I had of it too, you can well believe
it, Miss Stevie.'

James poured his mother and Beattie a glass of
sherry. Beattie drank hers off in a rush. 'Lunch will be
on the table in ten minutes. Will you show Miss Stevie
to her room, Jamie? She may want to freshen up a
little.' Beattie's orders were obviously to be obeyed,
and smiling at the two older women, James guided
Stevie out of the room; asked her to wait for a moment
while he fetched their bags, then led her up a wide
staircase.

'They're both absolutely lovely,' Stevie said with
feeling.

He squeezed her waist in response,

'Beattie will have made up the room next to mine,' he told her as he led her along a corridor.

'Knows your habits, does she?' Stevie couldn't keep herself from saying.

He pretended not to notice and carried on. 'She and Mother sleep at the opposite end of the house. There's a library over there. We don't use much more than that now.' A faraway look came into his eyes and then, after a minute, he shook his head as if willing memories away.

When he opened the door on to Stevie's room, she smiled with pleasure. A gabled window looked on to the rounded hills at the back of the house and an old gnarled oak. There was a large double bed, covered with a white Arran bedspread, pale blue walls, a small chest and dressing table, all tastefully arranged.

'We share the bathroom,' said James, pointing to another door and depositing her bag. 'Beattie means ten minutes when she says ten minutes, I should warn you.' Suddenly he looked at her with a searching gravity. 'Are you all right, Stevie? It's not too difficult for you?'

A lump rose to her throat and tears gathered in her eyes, making her pupils darkly luminous.

He was at her side in seconds, his arms round her, his lips nuzzling her hair. 'It means a great deal to me, Stevie.' His voice was a hoarse whisper. She clung to him, feeling desire whip through her like an arching flame only fanned further by the tenderness of his brief kiss.

'Eight minutes,' he warned, then left her.

Stevie thought the tears would overwhelm her. She leaned out of the gable window and took a deep breath of air, then with a 'Damn!' she hung up her few things in a rush and slipped into a pale lilac cotton frock whose tiny pleats made a mockery of creases. Her image in the small mirror looked innocently poised.

As she walked back down the stairs, she realised that

London seemed light years away. So much emotion had filled her two days with James that she found it hard to remember her life without him. Fool, she derided herself—You'll pay for this! But before she joined the others, she reminded herself that she intended to play her role to perfection.

'You look wonderfully pretty, my dear,' Mrs Reid greeted her as she came in.

'She always does, Mother.' James's eyes flickered over her, as he helped his mother out of her chair and with an arm around each woman led them to the dining room.

Beattie had spread plates full of cold meat and salad on the large oak refectory table that stood in the middle of the long room, rustic in flavour. She joined them in the late lunch and introduced spicy remarks into a conversation which largely served to catch James up with local gossip. Stevie noticed that Mrs Reid looked exceedingly tired by the end of the meal, and she was not surprised when James suggested that she go up to her room for a rest. Stevie offered to help with the dishes, an offer which Beattie gratefully accepted, and James vanished. 'He's off to see Stuart Buchanan,' Beattie informed her, 'to catch up on business.'

'So you're going to marry our Jamie?' Beattie asked while Stevie was drying a plate. Stevie almost dropped the dish, only catching it a second before it clattered out of her hands.

Beattie's bright blue eyes looked up at her wryly.

'Aye, lass, the thought of marriage is a frightening one. But I'm glad to see he treats you a sight better than those other lassies he's brought here on occasion.' She shook her head. 'Right terror, he can be. Didn't used to be, mind. It's grown worse these last years, since Alastair was killed in the car crash and we've had all the trouble.'

'Alastair?' Stevie queried, trying to assimilate all this information.

'Aye, his wee brother. Did he na' tell you? Terrible it was!'

Stevie tried to change the subject. Here, surely, was something she should have known about if she were to play her part effectively. And James had never mentioned a brother. She plied Beattie with questions about the farm, about the region, while she tried to make sense of what she had just learned. Did this brother have something to do with what she had so blithely called James's missing years? Might he explain some of those sombre thoughts, the traces of which she occasionally read on his face?

She promised herself she would confront him with it at the first opportunity. But the opportunity didn't present itself immediately. With James still absent, his mother resting and Beattie occupied, Stevie took a solitary stroll round the grounds, parts of which had been left to run wild, and into the woods with their bizarre imported trees. After a short walk she found herself by a small lake—a loch, she corrected herself— where she sat down and dipped her feet into the icy water. Indulging in reverie, she must have fallen asleep, for when she came to, the sun was already low in the sky. A wind had come up and Stevie clambered back to the house, arriving to find James and his mother sitting by a crackling fire.

'Stevie!' James looked at her in relief. 'I was just about to set up a search party.' He stood tall in cord trousers, a rough tweed jacket emphasising his broad shoulders. His worried air, his vital maleness, filled Stevie with a desire to touch him.

'Give him a kiss, my dear,' Mrs Reid urged, a smile on her face. 'He's been fretting like a caged tiger, but he didn't want to leave me.'

Shyly Stevie walked up to him and planted a kiss on his cheek. The slight roughness of his face, the cool tangy smell of him, made her pulses race, and she slipped out of his arms with the excuse that she had better change now that it had grown chill.

'Dinner is at eight,' Mrs Reid called after her.

Stevie went up to her room, forcing herself not to think, and lay in a hot bath for a few lazy minutes. Then slowly she began to towel herself dry. It was at that moment that she heard the door behind her open. She veered round and saw James standing in front of her. A devilish light flickered in his eyes and caught flame at the sight of her, her hair pinned on the top of her head, her rounded breasts, slender waist, long shapely legs. Stevie stood frozen into position for a moment, then she whipped her towel in front of her.

A low velvety laugh escaped him and in a moment he was upon her, his hands playing havoc with the skin of her bare back, his lips crushing hers into painful arousal.

'God, Stevie, how I want you . . . want you now!'

With a superhuman effort, she tore herself away from him and hurried towards her own room, trying simultaneously to cover her nakedness. He was right behind her and his hands caught her from behind, encircling her breasts and pressing her against his hardness. She could feel his heart pounding through her back while his lips rained kisses on her hair. Steeling herself, she turned to face him before he shattered all remnants of reason in her. She looked up at him, her eyes wide with seriousness, and said simply, 'No.'

'Why, Stevie? Why?' His voice was a caress that extended to the hand he trailed along her body. 'You want me—I've learnt enough about women to know that much.'

She shrugged away from him, twisting the towel carefully round her.

'Because,' she said gravely, and then smiled mischievously, 'Because dinner, laddie, is promptly at eight. And we can't keep your mother waiting.'

A hoarse laugh escaped him, but his eyes flashed wickedly. 'How silly of me, Ms fiancée!' He took her hand and delicately kissed the finger on which the emerald glowed. 'I'd quite forgotten my manners. But just wait until after dinner!' He tapped her playfully on the bottom and went back to his own room.

Stevie flung her towel on to the bed and herself down on top of it. 'This man is going to drive me stark raving mad,' she said aloud beating her fists on the pillows then she lay still, reflecting. What if she did make love with James? The thought of it made her heart beat wildly. 'No!' she said definitively, and bolted upright. No, she didn't want a little casual fling, no matter how wonderfully exciting. And she wouldn't get over a man like James easily Nor could she go back to Jordan then—Jordan, whom she had guiltily put off writing to for weeks—broken heart in hand, saying she would have him now that she had been tipped on the rubbish heap of the seduced and abandoned.

The thought made her cringe. It suddenly occurred to her that perhaps she had avoided those little round tablets of precaution all these years precisely so that she couldn't easily slip into the kind of temptation she was now experiencing.

Dinner, she reminded herself. Hastily she took out the one warm dress she had brought with her, a soft black woollen affair which was in fact a long jumper with puffed sleeves and rounded neck. She tied her wide green belt around her waist to dress the garment up a little, brushed her hair to a shining, gently waving mass and with a dab of eye make-up, she was ready.

James's eyes raked over her when she appeared in the drawing room. He had changed into a dark suit that gave him a commanding air, and as he stood to hand her a drink, his mother smiled warmly at them both. 'You will produce beautiful children,' she said.

A hot flush covered Stevie's face. It was so evident that Mrs Reid laughed.

'Give us a chance, Mother!' James groaned. 'At least a month or two. And stop embarrassing Stevie. You have to remember that she's a bit of a New England puritan—far worse than us Scots.'

'Nonsense,' his mother chided as he helped her out of her chair.

Dinner was a cheerful affair. Beattie had exerted herself to produce a fully Scots meal.

'Not the most varied cuisine in the world,' James noted, 'but when Beattie does it, it has its qualities.'

'Aye, that it does,' Beattie affirmed, placing a bowl of richly seasoned cock-a-leekie soup in front of Stevie. This was followed by a gaelic steak. 'Watch the whisky!' James warned. 'Beattie's generous with it when she stirs her sauces!' And the whole was topped with an oatmeal and fruit sweet which Stevie was told went by the name of Cranachan. Coversation flowed easily, and James was assiduous in his attentions to all the ladies.

Immediately after coffee in the drawing room, Mrs Reid retired, leaving James and Stevie sitting by the blazing fire. James drew his armchair closer to hers and reached for her hand, but Stevie pulled it away.

'You can stop pretending now,' she said sharply. 'We're quite alone.'

He looked at her, surprised. 'Is something wrong, Stevie?'

She rubbed her temples, feeling the strain of the day's events mounting into a headache. 'I'm getting tired of this theatre of tender love and care, that's all.'

He stood to his full height and began to pace the room, his face sombre. 'I didn't realise you were having to act so *very* hard,' he said in an insolent voice.

'I simply share you consummate talent,' she glared at him. 'Oh, Mother, stop embarassing Stevie; Oh, Stevie, I've been so worried about you!' she bounced up and began to imitate all his little gestures of consideration, her voice rising into hysteria.

He looked at her gravely. 'Yes, I can see you have a considerable talent.'

'And,' Stevie pressed on, 'you never told me about

your brother, and Beattie almost caught me out, and how am I supposed to be this beloved future wife of yours if I don't even know about things like that!'

'What did she tell you about Alastair?' James's voice cut into her barrage of words like a steel blade.

Stevie stopped. His eyes were like black gems glinting fiercely in the firelight. The tears rose to her eyes. 'Only that he was killed in a car crash,' she said in a small voice.

His hands, she saw, were clenched into tight fists. His face looked tortured, the eyes haunted with pain. 'I should never have allowed him to go,' he murmured.

'Do you want to tell me about it?' Stevie said softly.

He shrugged. 'There isn't much to tell. Alastair thought he was in love with some model he'd had a very brief affair with in London—wildly beautiful, he kept telling me. He kept ringing her up and finally she consented to see him again. He rushed up to London in a frenzy. Killed on the way. The woman never even came to the funeral.'

'So that's why you're so scathing about models,' Stevie breathed. She knew as soon as she had said them that the words were totally inappropriate to the moment.

He looked at her darkly. 'Wouldn't you be?'

She nodded, not wanting to contradict him, then added, 'But it's certainly not your fault in any way, no one's fault, really.'

He shrugged again. 'I could have stopped him. I should have. I knew that in that mood he would drive like a madman. But at the time I thought, why not? Wild oats and all that. I'd had mine.'

Stevie sat quietly for a moment sensing his grief. Then she asked, 'But why are you doing fashion photography now? A form of exorcism?'

'Perhaps, though not altogether.' He looked at her pensively. 'But this is no time for an interview. Go to bed, Stevie. You're obviously exhausted,' he ruffled her hair and gave her a fleeting smile.

'Goodnight,' she murmured, knowing he wanted to be left alone to gaze into the flames. Yet somehow she felt hurt at the dismissal, like an unwanted child. She scoffed at her earlier trepidation: there was no need for her to worry about James's attentions in his present mood. The words he called after her echoed her thoughts with a vengeance.

'And Stevie, I'll try to be less effusive in my marks of love tomorrow!'

Feeling irrationally and desperately hurt at this concession, Stevie went slowly up the stairs.

At breakfast the next morning, Stevie sat alone with Mrs Reid. James, she was told, had gone off early to work with Stuart.

'Do you think we might have a little heart-to-heart chat, my dear?' the older woman looked her straight in the eyes before pouring out more coffee.

Stevie nodded, trying to still her mounting nervousness.

'Do you love James very much?' Mrs Reid asked.

Stevie's stomach fluttered. 'Yes,' she answered honestly after a moment.

'Yes, I can see you do. And I know he loves you very much. I'm so pleased and so relieved, I can't tell you,' Mrs Reid smiled at her, warmth suffusing her grey eyes. 'After Alastair died, and after all that had gone before—you know, the wars and the battle fronts and his best friend being killed—I had this terrible sense that James would never feel any of the good, the simple things, properly again.' She looked at Stevie reflectively.

'He hasn't told me much about Alastair,' Stevie said.

'No, he wouldn't. He's very closed about himself. Give him time. You haven't known each other very long.'

'He is still depressed about him, though. He thinks it's his own fault,' Stevie pressed on.

Mrs Reid shrugged. 'James's sense of responsibility is

almost too well developed. You see, he loved Alastair almost like a father. Alastair was ten years younger then him, and we all spoiled him dreadfully. It's my fault as much as anyone's. I let Alastair run wild.' She was quiet for a moment, then she went on in a strangely remote voice.

'Some of one's children are weak, some strong. Alastair was the weak one. James saw him through school, through exams, got him out of scrapes. When he dropped out of university, James suggested that he take over the running of the estate. He ran it into the ground. James was working abroad a lot then and none of us really realised until it was almost too late. Mr Buchanan was too afraid of James's response to tell him the blatant facts. Things only became clear when James came back here for his extended rest, after he was wounded. He stayed on, took things in hand,' Mrs Reid's voice trailed off for a moment. She looked into the half distance and Stevie saw the pain written on her face as she continued.

'After Alastair was killed, we discovered he'd left enormous debts behind—gambling debts. James is still paying those off. I think that's partly why he started doing this fashion work, partly too, I suspect, though he's never said anything about it, because Alastair used constantly to tease him about only photographing horror, about being a boringly serious puritan.'

Mrs Reid's face brightened. 'In any case, that's all over now. We can settle back to some kind of normality.'

'I see,' Stevie breathed. All the pieces of the puzzle were suddenly falling into place.

Mrs Reid patted her shoulder. 'And when is the wedding to be, my dear? The sooner the better as far as I'm concerned, you know.'

Stevie blanched. 'We haven't set a date yet,' she managed to say—and then, feeling the woman's eyes steadily on her, added, 'My father will be in London soon and I wanted to wait until I'd told him face to face.'

Mrs Reid stood up. 'James is a good man, Stevie. I say it not only because he's my son. You'll be kind to him, won't you?'

Stevie nodded, feeling a lump rise in her throat.

'Getting to know each other a little better?' James strode into the dining room, bringing a tangy breath of the outdoors with him. 'Hello, love,' he brushed Stevie's hair with his lips.

'I'm afraid I've been doing all the talking,' Mrs Reid chuckled.

'I'm amazed that Stevie gives you a chance,' James teased her gently. 'She's rather a talkative sort.'

Stevie rose to the banter. 'I have to keep making up for all those thousands of words in each of your pictures.'

'I shall leave you children,' Mrs Reid smiled. 'I have letters to catch up on, now that I have some good news to convey.'

'Do you ride, Stevie?' James asked when his mother had left them.

Stevie's eyes sparkled. 'Are there horses?'

James groaned, 'I should have known! She swims, she rides, she talks, she . . .' his eyes flickered over her body wickedly.

'She doesn't,' Stevie gave him a playful slap . . .

'Not with anyone?' His eyes opened wide in mock astonishment.

'None of your business,' she laughed. 'Where are those horses?'

He gulped down some coffee while Stevie pulled on her boots, then led her to the stables. 'This is Bathsheba, she's for you. And this is Adam Smith.'

Stevie giggled at the assortment of names and patted the chestnut mare lovingly, while James saddled the horses.

They cantered off side by side, breaking into a gallop

as they reached open fields. There was a soft drizzle falling and with the wind in her face, the softly rolling countryside before her, Stevie suddenly felt a wave of pure joy flash through her. She glanced at James, the proud set of his head, the muscled shoulders beneath the thick sweater, the wild unruly hair, and burst out laughing. He shot her a quizzical glance. 'Marlboro country!' she shouted out at him.

'No, Scotland,' he laughed back, and nudging his horse galloped out in front of her.

By the time they got back to the house, they were both drenched. The devilish light was in his eyes again as he gazed at her glowing cheeks framed by the mass of honey-gold hair. When she dismounted, he caught her in his arms. 'Perhaps I really will marry you, if you can bring yourself to abandon this American of yours,' he said playfully.

Stevie stiffened visibly and he dropped his arms to his side, looking at her steadily for a long moment. Then he walked slowly away. 'You'd better go off and change. I don't want you sneezing into the camera lens,' he called over his back.

Stevie wanted to stop him, but no presentable words entered her mind. What did it matter? she consoled herself. He had in any event been joking.

The rest of the day passed quietly. After a pleasant enough lunch, James disappeared with the excuse of work. It was too wet to go swimming, as Stevie had hoped. She spent her time chatting to Mrs Reid or Beattie, who took her off to visit the rest of the house, while the other woman was resting. The unused rooms were a little musty, but seemed eminently usable.

'We open it up when the whole family comes to visit,' Beattie explained, pointing out that James's nephews and niece seemed to take up more space than an army.

It was only when Stevie went up to her room that she heard the sound of a typewriter through the library door and realised that James must be writing. She would have liked to browse through the books, but she didn't want to interrupt.

James must have heard her footsteps, for the door opened just as she passed it. 'Would you like to come in, Stevie? Perhaps we could do that interview now? I could use a break.'

Stevie gazed up at him in surprise. In all the barrage of emotion, she had all but forgotten the interview she was meant to do.

'Yes, of course,' she murmured. 'I'll just get my pad and the list of questions I drew up. The magazine suggested some as well.'

'What? No tape-recorder?' James looked at her sardonically. 'What kind of post-Watergate American are you?'

Stevie grimaced. 'A good one—and don't worry, I won't doctor the interview. Not unless this upright Scotsman asks me to,' she added ironically.

She went to fetch her notebook and returned almost instantly. He was sitting at a large desk, heaped with books and papers. Cigarette smoke filled the lofty well-proportioned room, with its book-lined walls. Stevie sat down a little nervously at the very edge of a leather chesterfield. James swivelled his chair round to face her, leaned well back into it and stretched his long legs in front of him. 'Fire away, Ms Henderson.' A teasing smile played over his face.

Stevie looked anxiously at her notes and then began by asking him about his work in the past. He answered her simply and directly, continuing to do so even when she asked about his reasons for changing his line of work and then his re-emergence as a fashion photographer. He told her about his trial run in Scandinavia where he had by chance begun working with Irena (some chance, Stevie flinched inwardly) and added, 'It makes a change to deal with at least the "gloss" of beauty.'

'Is there anything you feel you have to contribute to the fashion field?' Stevie queried.

He shrugged, 'Oh, I don't know. Time will tell. I'd like to break the code which says that models have to be staring over our heads into some hazy promised future of consumer goodies. Perhaps too, it would be interesting to extend the scope of types: we come, after all, in all sizes and shapes.'

Growing more daring as his good humour persisted, Stevie tried one of the questions the magazine had fed her. 'I know our readers would like to learn something about your own particular tastes in women? Can you tell us something about that?'

'Oh, I don't know.' James's eyes mocked her and carried out a flagrant inspection of her body, moving from her face down the length of her legs and slowly back again. 'I think I rather like them small, dark, slightly short sighted and a little plump. But the package is really rather irrelevant, wouldn't you agree, Ms Henderson?' He looked at her sardonically.

Stevie felt the warmth stealing into her face, but she pressed on, keeping her eyes well away from him.

'And are there any particular women in your life? Your name has been linked with that of the model Irena Borg, for one . . .'

A hushed silence fell over the room and when Stevie glanced at him, she saw that his face had darkened. She looked quickly down at her notepad and waited for what seemed an eternity. His voice when it came was harshly controlled. 'There are no particular women in my life, Ms Henderson. No particular women at all.' He stood to his full height and strode over to the window, which looked out on a grey sky.

Stevie tried to keep her dismay from showing in her face. She didn't know what she had expected him to answer to her question, but his tone, the cold finality of his words, had cut right through her. She averted her eyes from his and stood up, trying desperately to look casual. 'Thanks, James, I think this will do very well.'

He said nothing, simply continued to stare into the

dying daylight, and making herself as small as possible, Stevie walked towards the door. She hesitated on the threshold and looked back at him. He had turned now, but there was a preoccupied air on his face, as if his mind were quite elsewhere. Stevie's heart sank. So that was that. Tomorrow they would be off to meet the Americans and the little piece of romantic theatre would be over.

Holding her head high, she walked slowly towards her own room, and only when the door was safely closed behind her did she tumble down on the bed and let the tears flow. She had blatantly breached his code of privacy, she knew; and in the process she had found out something she would far rather not have known. The knowledge brought with it a pain that cut her quite in two. Its very intensity made her realise the extent of her love and how bitter life would be without it.

CHAPTER EIGHT

STEVIE kept her wide smile securely in place as she said goodbye to Mrs Reid and Beattie the following morning and thanked them profusely. No, she wouldn't come back with James on the return trip to London, she insisted again. Work called. But yes, she held her breath through the lie, she would visit again as soon as she could. She hugged both women and then waited in the car while James made his farewells.

'So you don't want to make the return journey with me?' he asked coldly after they had left the estate.

'I can't,' she lied, working to keep her voice steady. 'I really have to get back to work.'

'I see,' he said grimly. She noticed his jaw clenching. 'The amateur theatricals proved too much for you.'

Stevie shrugged. She had made her decision over dinner the previous evening. James had been as considerate, as visibly loving as ever, and the certainty that he was simply playing a role for his mother, that he didn't care for Stevie 'in particular', had made her realise that she couldn't spend another day in this house, let alone an entire weekend charade. She was simply falling deeper and deeper into the trap of loving him, loving all his gestures, his little marks of kindness, which had become as imprinted on her mind as his tall muscular body and proud face. Even now, as she stared fixedly out of the window at a landscape which grew increasingly dramatic with each turn in the road, she was so intensely aware of him that there was no need to look at him to sense his mood, the expression of his eyes.

They drove silently under a steel-grey sky which

138

seemed only to intensify the beauty of the spectacle nature had placed before them. For miles, its primordial stillness enveloped theirs, giving Stevie the sense that she was driving through infinity itself. At last James spoke, his voice cracking the air.

'I'd like to thank you, Stevie. It was good of you to see the whole thing through,' he said formally.

Tears stung Stevie's eyelids, but she kept her voice calm. 'If it has really cheered your mother, then I'm pleased. I don't know how you're going to ward off her questions about the wedding date, though.' A little high-pitched laugh escaped her.

'I've told her I'm totally at your disposal. And being one herself, she recognises that high-spirited women can't be pushed.' Stevie felt rather than saw the look he flashed her. 'In any case,' his voice took on a rough gravity, the doctors don't think it'll be much longer ...'

Stevie turned to look at him, 'I'm sorry,' she breathed softly. 'I liked her enormously.'

They drove silently until James suggested they stop for an early lunch. 'I think it's time I briefed you about all the wonders I expect from my new assistant.'

'When do I begin?' Stevie rubbed her hands in not altogether pretended glee, and he chuckled.

'Safely back in the neutral territory of work. That pleases you, does it?'

She nodded.

'Well, you may develop a distinct nostalgia for the halcyon days of Carn Laith by the time we're through. I'm not always the easiest of taskmasters.' His voice carried just a hint of menace.

'So I remember,' Stevie managed to reply archly, while she thought of the full extent of her feelings for James's home.

He laughed and pulled the car to a stop in front of a small village pub. He took several camera bags out of the car's boot and while they waited for lunch to be served, he showed her a variety of cameras and lenses, explaining which he would need to use for which purposes. Stevie's knowledge stood her in good stead. She had not been a camera buff for years to no purpose.

James smiled his pleasure at her quick grasp of things. 'The only other point to remember at all times,' he paused and looked at her sternly, 'is that I expect you to be at hand and to follow orders to a T.'

Stevie chuckled, 'I shall keep all my comments to myself and focus all my intelligence into my ears.'

'And your feet. There may be a bit of running around to do.'

'They're bringing plenty of their own staff,' she pointed out, 'apart from the models.'

'As long as they don't all have different ideas. That will be your job as well. You keep them entertained, while I get on with work.'

'At that rate, I could be off in Brazil with Tom Brewster,' she laughed.

He gave her a dark look. 'Selling your wares to captains of industry. Is that a way of life?'

Stevie was taken aback by the grimness of his response. 'That, Mr Boss Photographer, was a joke,' she flashed wide emerald eyes at him. 'Not,' she added softly, 'that what I do with my life concerns you in the least.'

He scowled at her, but the arrival of their waitress prevented any further reply.

They didn't arrive at their destination, a small hotel near Castle Urquhart, until late afternoon. James had insisted on what he called the scenic route, which took them through a magnolia-filled subtropical oasis and then an extraordinary national park where Stevie was amazed to see bison, ibex and wild horses keeping pace with the car. Her oohs and ahhs had kept James smiling and now, as she gazed into the depths of Loch Ness hoping to catch a glimpse of the monster, he let out a loud guffaw. 'The only monster you're bound to see around here is me—as soon as those Americans turn up.'

'The Genghis Khan of the fashion world turning on my compatriots,' Stevie teased.

James shook his head despondently. 'You'll have to get your geography right, Stevie. I can't possibly be Genghis Khan and ride through Marlboro country.'

Stevie looked up at him boldly, letting her eyes skim his length in slow motion. 'Oh, I don't know . . .' she said provocatively.

Their eyes met for an intimate moment.

James chided her, 'Just watch those looks, Ms Assistant, or by the time those Americans arrive, we'll be happily in bed together or one of us will be floating in the depths of the Loch.'

Stevie pretended to make ready to dive off the cliff, but his strong arms encircled her. 'No, you don't! Stay right there and pose for the camera. I need a practice session before the light vanishes and you need a few snaps for the family album. Uh-Uh,' he silenced her protests, 'assistants always do as they're told.'

Stevie watched him walk towards the car and sighed. Perhaps things wouldn't be so difficult now that they were working. If she could just keep her feelings at bay, then—well, then the banter would be not so very different from what it was with Anthony.

James returned with two cameras. 'Now amuse yourself and try to forget that I'm here.'

'That shouldn't be too difficult,' Stevie grumbled, and pulling her fingers through her wind swept hair, she went through a few comically exaggerated poses, before settling into more ordinary postures.

When they arrived back at the hotel, the lobby looked distinctly lively. Three wondrously tall slender women were leaning back against the reception counter surveying the room. They towered over a trim young man who was talking in a loud voice to the matronly receptionist.

'Watch your assistant move into action,' Stevie murmured to James. She walked over to the man, drew him into conversation and waved James over to introduce him. Andrew Dukes, the art director, explained that at the last moment they had decided on three models instead of two, and he presented them to a striking redhead with fierce grey eyes, a coolly elegant blonde with a trim new-wave hairdo, and a vivacious brunette. All three girls turned their attention immediately to James, who could then only give cursory greetings to the rest of the crew.

They all moved to the bar for a drink, where Dukes ushered James and Stevie aside to tell them that he had been scouting locations all day. With an exuberant flow of New Yorkese, he explained exactly what he wanted—elegance and contained romanticism, up-market folklore, he called it—and where he wanted it.

James listened intently, noted that they would have to start at daybreak—mists permitting—if they were to get the best light and avoid the possibility of rain, and suggested that if Dukes really wanted up-market folklore, they might consider a short drive to one particular stretch of the coast, which was far more dramatic than the Loch. 'There's a ready-made castle for you there, intact, not like this one,' James gestured in the direction of Castle Urquhart, 'and it happens to belong to my great-aunt.'

Dukes' eyes lit up at the suggestion. 'Great! You've got until Wednesday, Thursday at the latest if the weather is bad. Two days here should be enough. Then we can move on.'

From that moment Stevie was caught up in a flutter of activity. Dinner in the hotel restaurant passed in a blaze of sound as everyone at the table talked simultaneously. She had all but forgotten the pitch characteristic to such occasions in New York and she felt her head reeling with fatigue. James, she noted, despite his supposed distate of empty-headed models, seemed totally captivated by the three sirens who competed for his attention throughout dinner. The food tasted like sandpaper in Stevie's mouth and, pleading exhaustion, she retired to her room early. She felt disgruntled. James had barely noticed her leaving.

Rotton so-and-so, she thought to herself. But she fell asleep the minute her head touched the pillow.

She was woken at six-thirty the following morning and after a quick shower and a peep at the glimmering morning sun, she pulled on her jeans and went downstairs. The models were already there, dressed in their first assortment of clothes, rich tartans in a variety of shades, softly blending cloaks in thick wool and odd, perky little hats. They were just having the last touches of make-up applied to their faces and they looked strangely out of place in the homey hotel, like giant cardboard cut-outs, Stevie thought.

But she didn't have much time to think, for James's orders came fast and furious as soon as they stepped out of doors. It was as if he had forgotten that they had any relationship outside the professional, and Stevie was kept on the hop, following the odd group of players—as she called them to herself—from place to chosen place. The weather held, so they carried on for the rest of the day, stopping only for a late lunch of sandwiches and coffee. By evening, Stevie felt she couldn't stand another order or another face, and she escaped to the privacy of her room. When James's voice came through the door inviting her down for dinner, she was reluctant to leave the comfort of her bed. 'I'll be a few minutes yet,' she said.

'I'll meet you down there, then,' he called back. But by the time Stevie met him, he was engaged in what seemed a suspiciously intimate tête-à-tête with the redhead. Stevie chatted desultorily to Dukes and again escaped early.

The next day was a repetition of the first, with changes in costume and setting. Stevie wondered at her own lack of excitement, as she loaded roll after roll of film. 'I should be enjoying this,' she kept repeating to herself. But she knew she wasn't, and she was relieved when Dukes told her they would be heading off that afternoon to the castle James had named on the coast.

At least we'll have a quiet moment together in the car, she thought to herself as she hurried off to pack.

After a slight hesitation, she changed out of the jeans she had worn for the last few days, and dressed carefully in her elegant crushed-linen trouser suit, not admitting to herself that she was tired of going unnoticed amongst the models—even if that had been her own original decision. She examined herself in the mirror, feeling dissatisfied with her wide candid eyes, her clothes, herself. She was almost ready to change back into her jeans, when a female voice at the door warned her that departure was imminent.

She ran down the stairs two at a time, noticing that their four-car retinue was ready to set off with James in the lead. As she walked towards the car, she saw that the redhead was seated next to James. Her heart sank.

'Donna has asked if I would tell her something about the sights on the way,' James explained.

'I see,' Stevie said morosely. 'Do you want me to travel with the others?'

'Of course not, Stevie. There's plenty of room.'

Donna made no move to get into the back seat, so Stevie edged into it. Her temper was at boiling point and the girl's constant flirtatious chatter almost made it boil over. 'Do you think we might have some music, James?' Stevie asked after some thirty minutes of almost uninterrupted silliness.

'Oh yes, a Highland fling,' Donna giggled.

Stevie groaned inwardly. He doesn't even notice how ridiculous she is, they both are, she said to herself crossly. All this talk about disliking models, preferring plain, intelligent Janes, it's all a load of hogwash. She sat there fuming, her anger not even dispelled by the sight of the coastline and its breathtakingly jagged cliffs stretching right into the sea.

James pulled up in front of a gothic-spired building which seemed to have been converted into a hotel.

'We'll stop here,' he explained. 'It's large, so there shouldn't be any problem with accommodation.'

Stevie uncurled her stiff body from the back seat and thankfully left the car. She headed off towards the coast without sayng a word.

James called after her, 'We'll start work in a couple of hours, Stevie. I want to get some sunset shots in.'

She turned, nodded and then set off again, clambering down an incline towards the stretch of sandy beach. She took off her shoes, rolled up her trousers and paddled desultorily through the shallow water. The sound of the sea breaking, its rhythmic momentum, gave her a momentary sense of peace. One more day, she thought, and then it would all be over. The tears started to flow down her face and she let them fall, to be blown dry only by the wind.

She noticed, just a little way out in the water, an old shipwrecked hulk, strangely intact, despite the sea-worn wood. It seemed to beckon to her from a still centre in a forgotten time. Rolling her trousers up to her knees, she waded towards the vessel. She climbed on to the deck and after a little exploration sat down on the weatherbeaten boards and stared out to sea. The plash of waves against wood lulled her into a reverie. She felt totally alone, remote. No one in the world knew of her whereabouts. The thought filled her with a momentary rush of self-pity. She stilled it and tried to think sensibly of what she would do when she was back in London.

Her residue of guilt towards Jordan suddenly loomed large. She *must* write to him, explain that as warmly as she felt for him, he shouldn't place any hopes in her. With a fierce clarity, she knew now that her mother and Marissa were right, that she didn't care for Jordan, feel about him as a woman felt about the man she loved;

that no matter how much she might be hurt by cutting away from the security that Jordan provided, indeed how much *he* might presumably be hurt in the process, it would be a travesty of love, even of good faith, to marry him. She realised too that she had acquiesced to his wishes only partially because it suited her. In part she had also been simply too cowardly to say no, too cowardly to suffer his displeasure—like an adolescent who bends to the whims of popularity. It had been easier just to let things slide along. Stevie lay back on the damp deck and looked up into the sky. No—there was only one man in her life, even if he didn't want her.

She stood up, sad but firm in her resolution, her new-found knowledge which demanded immediate action. Something, at least *within* her, had crystallised.

When she walked round the deck to the shore side, she noticed that the tide had come up suddenly, that the beach was now much farther away than she had left it, and that the water looked menacingly deep, treacherous. She shivered. She would have to swim back. With a shudder, she kicked off her shoes and tying her jacket round her waist, lowered herself into the water. It was bitterly cold and took her breath away. Uttering a wordless prayer, she plunged in, gasping at the ferocity of the current, the icy waves. With a rising tide of panic, she realised that her strokes were bringing her no closer to the shore. She struggled against the undertow, against the mounting numbness in her limbs, the sudden overwhelming heaviness of her clothes. A large wave brought her under and when she came to the surface again, gasping for breath, another followed fiercely behind.

She flailed against the strength of the waves, fear gripping her with a devastating force. Just as she was about to go under for the third time, an arm encircled her, dragging her to the surface, and she heard a remote voice commanding her to lie still.

An eternity later, she was lying on the sand, her

throat raw with salt. She opened her eyes and saw James's head bent over her, his eyes dark with concern. For a moment she thought it was yet another image of him flitting through her mind. But the voice reassured her, as did the touch of his hand.

'It's all right now,' James murmured. 'I'll have you in bed with a hot water bottle in a jiffy.' He lifted her in his strong arms, as if she were a mere slip of a girl, and shielding her against the wind, carried her towards the hotel. Stevie clung to him, glad of the warmth of his body beneath the dampness of his shirt.

'Thanks for strolling by and rescuing me,' she tried to introduce a light note into her voice, but it broke. 'One more wave and I'd have been a goner!' She stared out to sea.

James's arms grew tighter around her. 'I thought you must have got into some kind of scrape when you didn't turn up for the session.' He held her eyes for a sombre moment and then scolded, 'Hasn't anyone warned you about exploring shipwrecks, about sea tides?'

Stevie didn't like being treated like a child. 'I'm better at lakes and rivers,' she said in a disgruntled tone, and pulled away from him.

But he clasped her even closer, putting her down only when they had reached the hotel, and then guiding her towards her room. He ordered her into a hot bath and immediatly to bed.

Stevie protested.

'If you don't do exactly as I say,' James threatened menacingly, 'I'll place you there forcibly myself!'

Stevie's eyes challenged him. 'You just try it, Genghis Khan!'

'Don't taunt me, Stevie.' He took a step towards her and tugged at her shirt, at one and the same time unfastening her trouser button.

Stevie raced away from him and locked the bathroom door shut. The sound of his laughter echoed after her.

She soaked in the steaming water, ate the dinner

James had had sent up and found that she was indeed
as exhausted as he had predicted. As soon as her head
hit the pillow, sleep enveloped her.

She woke with a start to the shrill sound of female
laughter which seemed to be coming through the walls
from the room next door. In the few seconds that it took
her to remember where she was, she heard another
sound: this time it was a man's voice, its tones deep and
warm. The voices suddenly crystallised into familiarity
and Stevie recognised James and Donna. A shock went
through her as she realised what these two mingled
voices suggested and a pit seemed to open in her
stomach. She steeled herself against the on rush of tears
and lectured to herself in a severe tone: Stop it, Stevie!
You knew it would be like this. He's been playing with
you, that's all. Perhaps he even cares for you in a
friendly way, but no more than that. Let it be. Luckily
it isn't worse.

Mentally she lifted her shoulders back and threw her
head high. At least James would never know how she
felt about him, never recognise the depth of her
attachment.

With a sudden sense of compulsion, she got up and
rifled through a bureau drawer. Yes, there was some
writing paper. She took it to bed with her and propping
herself against the pillows, began a letter to Jordan. It
was time to follow through her resolution, to be honest
with him. It would be far too easy to slip back into a
habitual security, to shy away from honesty, now that
her foreboding about James had materialised into a
distinct reality. She must do the right thing.

Avoiding as best she could the sound of the voices
from the room next door, she forced herself to write a
long letter and explain as best she could how she had
realised that much as she cared for Jordan, it wasn't in
a way that paved the path to marriage. She explained
that another man had made her see this, though in no
way should Jordan feel that he had been abandoned for

someone else. This other man—Stevie gripped her pen fiercely—had merely clarified things for her, made her realise that perhaps she was using Jordan. She signed the letter, 'With continuing and deep affection, Stevie.'

Wednesday dawned bright and clear and despite her sense of inner bleakness, Stevie prepared herself to act as professionally as possible. She even felt a little surge of excitement as she drove with James and Donna along the breathtakingly beautiful coastline towards James's promised castle. Yet the exhilaration passed all too quickly. After a brief hello to James's aunt, work took over, and Stevie could not but be aware of Donna's increasingly overt gestures of friendliness towards James. Just a little longer, she drilled herself, and then she'd be away, away from this man and the constant irritant of his presence.

That evening, their last, Stevie bought some postcards and sat quietly in the hotel lobby writing to friends. She felt James approaching even before she saw him. They hadn't had a moment alone all day and she suddenly felt acutely nervous. He sat down beside her, stretching his long legs lazily in front of him. She looked up at him. His face was tired, his eyes sleepy as they met hers.

'Feeling well enough to reaffirm your contacts with the real world?' he asked, a hint of the sardonic in his voice.

Stevie nodded. 'It feels centuries away.'

James laughed, a low rumbling sound, then scanned the cards and the single letter on the table. Suddenly his eyes looked troubled. 'Jordan. Jordan Richards. Is that his name?' he challenged her.

'Whose name?' Stevie asked innocently.

'The man back home,' he brought it out insolently.

She nodded defiantly, suddenly wanting to hurt him if she could. 'And he's the best man I know.'

'Do you miss him very much?' James asked, his voice low.

'Very much,' she agreed.

'Then why aren't you with him now?' He pressed her.

'We said we would have a year apart to taste a little of other lives.'

'I see,' he said tightlipped. 'And this, all this, is other lives,' he swept the room with a mocking glance.

'I guess so,' Stevie replied. 'They don't seem all that wonderful, do they?' Her eyes landed deliberately on Donna, who had just walked into the lobby.

James looked at her with such penetrating appraisal that she was forced to cast her eyes down. Then he said causually, 'Come and have dinner, Stevie. You look as if you could do with some sustenance.'

The dinner table was filled with the usual cacophony of voices, and once again Stevie excused herself early. She said formal goodbyes to the Americans who were leaving for the airport early the next morning—not a moment too soon, she thought to herself—and went up to her own room. She ran a leisurely bath, trying to soak the fatigue out of her limbs, slipped into a nightdress and was about to climb into bed when a knock sounded at the door.

Her heart set up a wild staccato rhythm, quite oblivious to the cautionary voice of her good sense. It must be, it could only be, James. She opened the door shyly.

Instead of James, she saw a waiter carrying a tray with a bottle of champagne in an ice-bucket. 'Thank you,' she said, gesturing him towards a table and trying to keep the tears from mounting to her eyes. She was about to close the door behind him when she saw James hurrying towards her down the corridor.

'I thought you might invite me in for a drink.' His eyes challenged her.

'Why not?' she met him on it. 'It's our last night here. Though I'm hardly decent.' She was suddenly aware of her flimsy shift which did nothing to hide the curves of her body as his gaze raked over her.

'The lady's already forgotten that I've seen her in far less decent attire,' he shook his head mockingly as he popped the champagne cork and poured them each a glass of bubbly liquid.

He raised his glass to her. 'Here's to the best assistant I've ever had—apart from any incidental drownings.' His eyes teased her and then grew serious. 'My thanks.'

Stevie lowered her eyes away from his face and sipped a little of her drink. Then she turned her back on him to look out on the moonlit landscape. The tide of yearning his presence in the intimate space of the room awakened in her needed to be restrained.

He was suddenly behind her, painfully close, his lips nuzzling her hair as his arms rose to embrace her, to cup her breasts and stroke her gently. 'Work is over, Stevie,' he said in a muffled voice. 'We can relax, be ourselves again.'

Despite herself, she trembled against him and his mouth shivered over her skin, raining kisses on the delicate flesh of her nape, as he held her more tightly to him. A molten flame shot through her, making her forget all caution, and she turned in the circle of his arms to reach for his lips. They kissed with an urgency of passion and tenderness that left her heart galloping with the thunder of a hundred horses.

James pulled her down into his lap on the broad armchair beside her window, so that the moonlight played over both their faces. Taking her hand in his, he fingered the ring which had weighed so heavily on her over the last few days, though she hadn't been able to bring herself to part with it.

'Stevie, are you sure you won't drive back with me tomorrow and stop over at the house again?'

She looked at the chiselled granite of his face, the dark eyes glimmering with reflected moonlight. 'I can't, James,' she said, her heart in her mouth. 'I can't pretend.' Swallowing hard, she pulled the ring off her finger with an unsteady gesture and handed it to him.

He looked at her gravely, shaking his head. 'No, I want you to keep it. It's yours, Stevie.' He all but pushed her off his lap and stood up brusquely. She thought he was about to leave and panic filled her, making the blood pound savagely in her temples. She put out a restraining hand and their eyes met in charged intimacy. He began to pace the room, like a trapped animal, turning on her suddenly, his eyes smouldering lights in his dark face. 'If you want that ring to take on meaning, Stevie, just let me know. It's up to you.'

She looked at him, her face luminous with astonishment. A strange voice croaked out of her, 'What?'

'You heard me, Stevie.' His laugh was menacing. 'If you change your mind about that Jordan of yours, decide you want me, *really* want me, let me know.' He turned on his heel.

Stevie reached him just as he was at the door. 'James,' her voice quavered, 'are you saying—are you asking me . . .?'

'What do you think I'm saying?' he thundered at her, and then, turning, he swept her up in his arms, crushing her to him, claiming her lips with such force that she thought they would never be her own again.

'Oh, Stevie, I want you to marry me,' he whispered, his voice rough with emotion.

She stared at him, her eyes wide, her body trembling with an ecstasy which could find no expression in words. He looked at her in her white slip of a nightdress, her hair tumbling around her face. 'It's all right, darling. You don't have to say anything now. But soon. Please make up your mind soon. I've had enough of this ghostly loyalty, this childish game-playing.' He passed a hand tenderly through her hair and slipped out of the room.

Stevie flung herself down on the bed, not daring to pinch herself for fear she would awake. Her body hummed like a harp, trilled to the music he had instilled in her, and to herself she sang, yes, yes, yes!

She woke with the word on her lips and hurried herself into her clothes with a haste which could only be put to rest by James's presence. Had she dreamt it all? She all but flew into the breakfast room. He was sitting alone at a small corner table and when his eyes lighted on her, a flood of such vibrant emotion filled her that she thought her legs would never carry her to the end of the room.

'Hello, Stevie.' He was looking at her dreamily.

Suddenly she had to know, had to hear him say it again in the clear light of day. She sat down, feeling awkward, her tongue clumsy in her mouth. 'James, yesterday—last night, did you . . . did you propose to me?' She brought out the word like a leaden weight.

'Well, it sure as hell wasn't a proposition, or I never would have left your room,' his blue-grey eyes mocked her.

A dreadful thought planted itself in her mind. 'Like Donna? I won't be part of a harem, you know.'

A flicker of anger lit his eyes, but it was dissipated in a comic groan. 'And here I thought you respected my taste, Stevie. My judgment.' He shook his head balefully. 'No, you'll never do as a wife.'

Her face fell.

'Silly!' He pressed her hand, kissing the finger which still wore its emerald. 'You remember every word I said distinctly, so stop pretending otherwise, because I don't propose every day. And I expect an answer *soon*. Not immediately. I want you to be sure, very sure, Stevie.' He searched her eyes for a moment and then added threateningly, 'But *soon*! Genghis Khan can't be kept waiting.'

They burst into mutual laughter.

The drive to Inverness, where Stevie was to catch the plane James had insisted she take back to London, passed all too quickly for Stevie. She asked herself why she didn't simply say she would go to Carn Laith with him, despite the fact that he wanted to give her time to make up her mind. There was, after all, no burning need for her to be in London. But as she thought about it, Stevie realised that James was probably right. It would probably be best for her to have just a little time to herself to absorb this sudden change, to assimilate all the emotions which raced wildly through her. She stole a shy glance at James, his taut muscled body and rugged profile behind the steering wheel. When had he decided he wanted her for good?

A thought cut through her with razor sharpness. He hadn't said he loved her. Perhaps he was doing all this for the same reason he had suggested their mock engagement: simply to please his mother. When he stopped the car, she confronted him.

'Is this—all this—on your mother's behalf, James?' she asked, her voice almost inaudible.

He looked at her askance and then drew her to him in a searching kiss which seemed to probe her very depths. His eyes sparkled as he released her. 'That too, Ms Stevie Henderson, was for my mother. Shall I show you what else I can do on her behalf?'

Stevie laughed, all worry suddenly far from her mind.

'And don't forget—I'm not a patient man!'

With radiant eyes and racing heart, Stevie looked at the man beside her. What did all her questions matter, what did anything matter, as long as she could spend her days and nights with him forever?

Back in London, she bubbled into the flat. Her eyes were glowing, a little smile hovering over her wide lips.

'My little pussycat has just swallowed two plump canaries.' Marissa eyed her quizzically, 'Out with it little sister, what have you been up to?'

'Oh, it's wonderful, just too wonderful!' Stevie sang.

'Well, start from the beginning. No, first ring Mother, she's decided on a flash party on Sunday and she wants to know whether you'll come and bring

James Reid. There'll be some people there it could be useful for him to meet.'

Stevie telephoned her mother, said she didn't think James would be back from Scotland in time, but she would certainly invite him if he were. Her mind danced at the thought, and then, thrilling to her news, she sat down to tell Marissa all about it.

Marissa hugged her sister. 'If that's what you want, Stevie——' she examined her carefully—'and I can see that you do,' she said after a moment, 'it's too wonderful for words. I can't wait to meet this Genghis Khan of yours.'

'You will, Marissa, you will!'

'As long as it proves less dismal than my last experience with a Reid,' said Marissa under her breath. But Stevie wasn't to be deflected at the moment by any consideration of Marissa. She waltzed off to bed and all but floated through the next few days. She couldn't quite assimilate the fact that James was now a reality in her life, a reality with a future. But her own buoyant joyousness reassured her, the trembling anticipation that suddenly came over her at odd moments.

When she sat down to work on her interview with him, to shape it into publishable form, a little tremor went through her. She paused over her last questions and his response—'No woman in particular'. With a shrug, she left it out. It was a silly thing to have asked him in any case, and she wouldn't have done it without prior instruction from the editor.

On Sunday morning Stevie had just finished washing her hair when the telephone rang, and Marissa called, 'It's for you, Stevie.'

Stevie picked up the receiver and heard James's deep tones at the other end. 'Stevie, I'm back—couldn't stay away from you any longer. I've been driving all night. Have you made up your mind?'

A warm tide coursed through Stevie's veins, making

her laugh strangely hoarse. 'Not yet,' James,' she teased, 'Maybe, maybe in about ten minutes or so.'

'Witch!' he breathed down the telephone.

She told him about her mother's party, said she would meet him there since she was going early to help out with preparations.

'Right, I'll catch a few hours' sleep, then. See you soon, darling.'

Stevie had only just put down the phone when it rang again. She picked it up, sure that it would be for Marissa who was hovering behind her; but the voice, oddly familiar yet distant, asked for Stevie Henderson.

Suddenly Stevie blanched. There was no mistaking Jordan Richards. She made a quick mental calculation. He couldn't have received her letter yet, she worked out—just as Jordan announced that he was ringing not from the U.S.A., but from London. He had been asked by a colleague to stand in for him at a conference in Cambridge. So here he was at the Cumberland Hotel. Could they meet immediately? He would have to be off to Cambridge in the morning.

Stevie tried to take all this in and still answer Jordan with welcoming excitement in her voice. Of course she had to see him, but she couldn't let her mother down, and she had already arranged to meet James at the party. There was nothing for it but to invite Jordan as well. She did so in what she hoped was not too shrill a tone.

'We can slip away early,' Jordan suggested. Your mother won't mind—and we've so much to catch up on.'

'Yes,' Stevie mumbled, and trying to sound bright, gave him her mother's address and instructions on how to get there.

'Trouble?' Marissa asked, as Stevie put the telephone down.

Stevie nodded and explained.

Marissa laughed mischievously. 'And of course you

haven't told him about James . . .' She shook her head, as if scandalised. 'And here I've always thought of you as my virtuous, fine-minded younger sister!'

Stevie bridled. 'I did write to Jordan from Scotland, but he hasn't received the letter yet.'

'Never mind, Stevie,' Marissa reassured her. 'It's sometimes best to do these things radically. And I'll help you out. I'll woo Jordan's thoughts away from you. If that's what you want,' she added, a hint of cattiness in her voice, 'otherwise, I can concentrate my wiles on James.'

'Just keep your hands off him, Marissa,' Stevie warned,

Marissa smiled. 'I'm only testing, Stevie—to see whether you really have made up your mind.' She hugged her sister. 'I *am* pleased for you—and don't worry, we'll manage the evening somehow.'

CHAPTER NINE

'Most certainly I have the two most beautiful daughters in the world,' Susannah Henderson gazed at Stevie and Marissa warmly. They had just finished changing into the party clothes they had brought with them to their mother's Kensington flat. Marissa had insisted that Stevie borrow one of her dresses, and she had chosen a rich plum off-the-shoulder silk that swirled round her hips, while Marissa donned a slightly rakish dusky rose shift in the softest suede.

Amidst all the preparatory bustle, Stevie had been too shy to take her mother aside and tell her about James, though she had explained as casually as she could about Jordan's sudden arrival. Her mother had only given her one quizzical look and brushed the matter aside. Stevie was glad now that she had decided to take her ring off—though at the time the act had filled her with a physical sense of separation. There was too much to catch her mother up on, and there would be plenty of time to do so, once she had actually met James. Stevie sighed happily to herself as the time for his arrival approached and she was suddenly filled with confidence. Everything would sort itself out in due course.

The guests began to arrive, her mother's usual blend of literati and media people, women in outlandish versions of vogue punk, men in sleek suits, all chatting away as if the act of speech were their primary business. Stevie stayed close to the door, keeping an eye out for James and Jordan. The latter arrived first, and Stevie took in his boyish athletic form, the blond fringe which needed constantly to be fingered aside, with a mixture of pleasure and embarrassment. He embraced her shyly, whispering to her that she looked more beautiful than ever. But before he had a chance to engage her in anything akin to personal conversation, Marissa swooped down on them and with consummate showmanship displayed her pleasure at seeing him on this side of the Atlantic. Jordan looked slightly bewildered and Marissa winked an aside at Stevie before she dragged him away to say hello to her mother. 'You'll have plenty of time to talk to Stevie later,' Stevie heard Marissa say, before her eyes focussed on a presence that made her oblivious to everything.

James had just walked into the room. As she looked across at him and took in his slow, lazy smile, the bristling crop of dark hair, the trim dark suit which seemed to emphasise the breadth of his shoulders and his natural grace, Stevie was intensely aware of his devastating magnetism. All eyes seemed to be on him as he strode over to her and brushed her forehead with light lips. 'You look good enough to eat,' his eyes flickered over her devilishly, 'and I'm ravenous! Shall we sneak away early?'

Stevie felt her skin tingle at his proximity, all her senses bounded to life and she laughed up at him wickedly. 'Come and meet my beautiful mother first. You may change your mind about leaving.'

He wound his arm around her waist. 'Shall we announce the good news?'

Stevie handed him a glass of champagne, 'I haven't had a chance to tell Mother about you yet. And besides,' she threw him a long teasing look, 'I haven't quite made up my mind.'

He gripped her waist with a new ferocity. '*Now*, Stevie,' his voice beneath the easy smile held a trace of menace. 'Say yes now, or I shall be forced to embarrass everyone here by kissing it out of you.'

Stevie flushed and was about to mouth her answer when her mother's voice intruded upon them.

'And who is this stranger who can bring the sparkle

into my daughter's eyes?' Susannah Henderson surveyed them both archly and stretched a hand out to James. Stevie introduced them.

'I've just been trying to persuade your daughter to run off with me,' James bantered as his eyes set fire to Stevie's cheeks, 'but now that I've met you, I think we can stay a while. You did warn me, Stevie!'

Stevie could see her mother carrying out a covert appraisal of James and she knew that within minutes, as his banter turned to seriousness, he had won her over. It was not something Jordan had ever been able to do. But then nothing he ever said seemed to interest her mother for more than a minute. She guessed it was James's presence, the very weight, the intensity he put into every gesture, every word, which captivated her mother as much as herself. Beside him, Jordan, for all his niceness, was nondescript. Stevie smiled blissfully to herself. If she wasn't careful now, she would lose James to her mother and to a round of introductions which would last the entire evening.

'Do stop monopolising James, Mum,' Stevie teased her mother. 'I want him to meet Marissa.'

Susannah Henderson smiled at them both. 'It's not often my daughter presents me with new faces I'd like to see more frequently. So do come again, Mr Reid.' She waved them away, only pulling Stevie aside for a moment to murmur, 'Now there's a man who would be a man to you, Stevie.'

Stevie looked at her with pretended shock, 'Really, Mother, you shouldn't go around matchmaking!' and then, with a little laugh, she returned her attention to James. 'I think she's taken to you,' she said lightly, not wanting to bely the bounding sense of excitement she felt every time she met his eyes. 'And now for the other woman in the family. But I won't stand for any harem-like gestures,' she warned him.

James took her hand and squeezed it. 'I don't promise anything until I've heard you say yes, loudly and clearly.' He stroked her fingers and then his tone changed abruptly. 'I see you've taken off the ring.' His voice was rough.

'Because of my mother,' Stevie began to explain, and stopped mid-sentence. She had just noticed Tara Alexander standing next to Marissa and Jordan, and her heart skipped a beat. The last time she had seen the raven-haired woman had been on the night when she had fled from James's house like a rejected child.

'It really is rather more important that we talk than that you introduce me to my editor.' There was a touch of impatience in James's voice.

'Another member of your harem, you mean,' Stevie replied, not knowing what had induced her to say the words.

James stopped and made her turn to face him. 'The woman's decidedly jealous,' he said after a moment, and his eyes twinkled at her. 'Wonderful Stevie, I won't give up all hope just yet.'

Stevie shot him a scathing look.

'Where is this wonderful sister of yours, then?'

'She's talking to an old friend of mine from the States,' Stevie answered, hesitation evident in her voice, the flush creeping into her cheeks. Then, steeling herself, she led James towards Jordan and Marissa.

'Jordan Richards, James Reid,' Stevie introduced the two men, trying to keep her voice even.

James threw her a questioning glance that turned into black disapproval before he took Jordan's hand. In the sudden tension of the moment, Marissa attempted a conciliatory explanation.

'Jordan has just arrived from the States today. He's an old family friend,' she stressed.

'Stevie seems to have a great many friends.' There was a harsh note beneath James's bland words.

'But only one sister, I can assure you,' Stevie jumped in, trying to hide her discomfort in banter. 'Though that one is the world's loveliest model. James, meet my sister Marissa Carr.'

Marissa stretched out her hand and smiled at James. He looked at her in utter amazement for a full minute and left her hand dangling in mid-air.

'Marissa Carr?' he repeated, as if transfixed.

Stevie saw a look of acute pain flicker over his face, only to disappear into momentary confusion. Then, scowling, he turned abruptly away with a barely audible, 'Excuse me. There's something I've just remembered I have to attend to.'

'I thought Englishmen were supposed to be the epitome of gentlemanly politeness,' Jordan shook his head behind James's retreating back.

'Ah, but James Reid is hardly the typical Englishman.' Tara Alexander, having watched their little scene, intervened. 'Any woman will tell you that,' she looked meaningfully at Stevie.

Stevie gave her a hostile glance, but was too stunned to speak.

'James is just suffering from one of his moods, I imagine,' Tara continued knowingly. 'He's rather prone to them.' And with that she flounced off to follow him.

Stevie barely took in Jordan's, 'And good riddance to them both. Now at last we can have a chance to talk.' She wanted to fly after James, but her pride held her back. Yes, it had been silly not to warn James more adequately of Jordan's presence, but for him to be so rude to Marissa in turn was inexcusable. He was talking to Tara Alexander now, and after a moment the woman wove her way back towards them.

'James has asked me to tell you he isn't feeling well. I'll see him home. Make our excuses to your mother, will you, Stevie.'

Stevie looked at her askance. Across the crowded room, she caught James's eye. His face was grimly set, the strong jaw determined. A frown creased his forehead, and he seemed to be staring right through her. The look signalled an infinite distance between them. Stevie's legs grew weak.

'He does look ill.' Marissa took Stevie aside for a moment to comfort her. 'We'll ring him in a little while to find out what's up.'

'No,' Stevie said stubbornly. 'He could have spoken to me himself. He's behaved inexcusably!'

Jordan came up to the two girls. 'Will you let me steal Stevie away now, Marissa? We need a little time to ourselves.' Marissa looked at her sister and Stevie nodded. Her emotions were in a jumble. She felt angry, confused, trapped. She knew she had to speak to Jordan, but now that everything was crumbling around her, her resolve to do so was evaporating. Listlessly, she let herself be guided by him and said her goodbye to her mother, who looked after her questioningly.

They went to a French restaurant nearby and sat facing each other in silence for a moment. Jordan was watching her as a man watches a woman and not with the ease of long-time friendship. It intensified Stevie's guilt, but she didn't know how to begin to explain her position.

At last he said, 'London suits you, Stevie, though I can't say I'm impressed by your friends.'

Stevie was about to leap to James's defence when she realised that there was nothing to say. She disapproved of his behaviour as much as Jordan did. Inside herself she panicked as she sought for some explanation, but on the surface all she could do was shrug. She turned the conversation to Jordan and his activities over the last months. He talked willingly enough, but after a while he stopped. 'Stevie, you haven't listened to a word I've said.'

Stevie looked down on the uneaten food on her plate. 'I'm sorry, Jordan. I'm trying to think of a way of saying what I know I have to say.'

He looked at her bleakly. 'Out with it, then. I've been expecting something.'

Stevie twisted and turned her words, but finally she managed to make herself clear enough.

'What you're saying is that you don't love me, don't want to marry me,' Jordan jumped in grimly. 'I suspected as much when I didn't hear from you for a while.'

'I wrote to you,' Stevie interrupted, 'but you wouldn't have received the letter before you left.'

'Who's the other man?' Jordan asked point blank, looking into her eyes.

Stevie shivered and then, as coolly as she could, she shook her head. 'I don't really know that there is anyone else.' The truth of her words emerged to her as she said them and seemed to cut her in half.

Jordan looked at her dubiously. 'I find that hard to believe.'

'Suit yourself,' Stevie shrugged.

He searched her face. 'Well, if there really isn't anyone else, then there's hope for me.'

'It's not like that, Jordan,' Stevie pleaded now. 'We're friends. I hope that never changes. But as for the rest—well, we know each other too well.'

'I don't think we know each other at *all*,' he said decidedly. He called for the waiter, paid their bill and hailed a cab as soon as they were outside. Once seated, he tried to draw Stevie to him and only managed to plant a clumsy kiss on her cheek.

Stevie pulled away. 'No, Jordan, that's what I mean. It isn't like that.'

'What you mean is you're still afraid of sex,' he said bluntly.

She let it pass. A sense of hopelessness overcame her. She realised that Jordan was right about the Stevie of six months ago—but as for now, it was all different. Her stomach turned painfully as she thought of James. But Jordan didn't want to understand and she couldn't explain without insulting him. Only the excuse or the reality of another man would deflect him. That was something he would understand, she thought bitterly.

They drove to Hampstead without speaking, and it was only with the promise that they would meet again on another evening when he came up from Cambridge that Stevie managed to extricate herself. She tried to leave on a friendly note, realising all at the same time that she was simply perpetuating the pattern which had always made her want Jordan's approval. 'I am very pleased to see you, Jordan, really,' she said.

He scowled, the look peevish in his youthful face. 'You have an odd way of showing it!'

She kissed him quickly on the cheek and ran up the stairs, pausing at the top in confusion. The shock of James's sudden shift suddenly hit her. What could she do now?

Marissa was waiting up for her. Her various attempts to cheer Stevie served little purpose.

'I can't understand how James's manner can change so radically from one moment to the next,' she said to Marissa, a hint of bitterness in her voice as she tried to hide her humiliation.

'Men!' Marissa breathed, throwing her arms up into the air. 'But you should ring him, if only to take him up on what you call his blatant lie of illness.'

Stevie shook her head.

'I think he's worth it, Stevie,' Marissa said softly, 'despite his rudeness. He doesn't look like the type who does things for no good reason, and he can't suddenly have stopped caring for you.'

Finally Stevie telephoned, almost hanging up when she heard a woman's voice at the other end of the line. But Marissa made her ask for James.

His voice, when it came, was flat, lifeless.

'Are you not feeling well—are you ill, James?' Stevie tried to keep her tone even, despite the butterflies in her stomach.

'No—yes,' he paused. 'Stevie, forget everything we've talked about.' His voice betrayed a hoarseness, but he spoke brusquely. 'Just forget about me and go off with your Jordan.'

Stevie's mouth dropped.

'I'm sorry—sorry for being rude, sorry for everything,' she heard him murmur almost inaudibly. And then the click announced an empty silence that echoed unendingly in Stevie's heart.

Despite Marissa's entreaties that she stay home, Stevie went to work on Monday, forcing herself into an activity which could at least momentarily keep her mind from turning the same dismal ground over and over.

Anthony took one look at her pale, swollen-eyed face and advised her to go straight back home.

'It's just a bout of hay fever,' Stevie mumbled.

He looked at her intently and queried her about the week in Scotland, but she kept her eyes glued to her desk, only saying as evenly as possible that it had gone well enough. Sensing her resistance, Anthony avoided the subject, indeed anything personal, for the rest of the day.

Stevie tried to work, but she knew that it was an empty pretence, that she was only waiting for James to ring, to offer some explanation for his behaviour, to make at least a sign. But there was no word from him that day or the next. Caught in a pendulum which swung from anger to bitter desperation and back again, she somehow stumbled through the hours.

Late on Tuesday afternoon, a flustered Mr Brewster came into their office.

'Can you explain what's going on, Stevie?'

She looked at him incomprehendingly.

'I've just had James Reid on the telephone politely explaining that although you've done excellent work for him and he's very grateful, he's withdrawing from the agency. When I asked him why, all he said was that he wanted to work at his own pace.'

With a gigantic effort of the will, Stevie kept her tears back. James had broken the last necessary tie. 'He's a strange man,' she managed to say in a small voice as she looked past Mr Brewster at the wall of files.

Mr Brewster eyed her severely, but when he saw that no further explanation was to come, he shook his head and turned to leave, stopping only to say, 'Well, at least Reid has been fair. He's said the agency should continue to draw a percentage on any work which comes to him over the next few months.'

'Are you going to tell me what happened?' Anthony asked as soon as Mr Brewster had shut the door behind him. 'This doesn't sound in the least like a professional squabble.'

The tears were now evident in Stevie's eyes. 'I don't know,' she mumbled. 'I simply don't know. One minute he was all kindness and light,' she lowered her eyes from Anthony's and paused, shivering at the memory, 'and the next he up and turned on me.'

'Well, I'm going to find out if I can,' Anthony determined. 'No one behaves like that without reason.' He picked up the telephone and a few seconds later, Stevie overheard him making a date to see Irena. She stood by passively, unable to make herself stop him, despite her rising sense of humiliation at the thought that she was going to become the subject of gossip— Irena's gossip at that.

'We're both going to have lunch with Irena tomorrow,' Anthony announced when he had hung up.

Stevie blanched. 'Oh no!' she wailed.

'Would you prefer to stay behind and have fantasies about what we're saying? I'm not blind or stupid, Stevie. I know you're head over heels with Reid, and it always makes things difficult professionally. But I would have thought he'd stick with the code. He didn't strike me as a man who did underhand things.'

'He's not,' Stevie jumped in to agree. She remembered how at one of their first meetings James had stressed that he didn't like the mix of business and pleasure.

'Well, I want to know what's going on—from a professional perspective as well as because of the look on your face. I can't bear having you drag yourself round this office like some outcast from the half-dead. And that's because of the almighty Reid, isn't it?'

Stevie nodded.

'Tomorrow at one, then.'

'Yes, all right, if we must,' Stevie acquiesced. 'But please, Anthony, you'll treat my private life discreetly?'

'I'm an honourable man, Stevie, didn't you know?' Anthony teased, and with a wink he turned away to work, only adding, seconds later, 'And Stevie, can we try an occasional smile? The atmosphere in here is oppressive.'

Stevie did her best, but the smile felt as if it had been painted on her face by an inept hand. Her despair was growing roots inside her. James's volte-face became more incomprehensible, the more she thought about it. Even if he felt that Jordan's sudden appearance meant that she preferred him to James, it wasn't in character for him to cut her so completely dead—and to leave the agency as well. She reflected on the possibility of jealousy, but jealousy would mean that he cared for her, and his words on the telephone belied that. Her thoughts always led her to a dead end in which only the simplest explanation worked: James had simply changed his mind about her and cut off all ties. Her blood ran cold, making her shiver perceptibly. The very hopelessness of that forced her to look forward to the meeting with Irena with something akin to anticipation.

Stevie and Anthony were already seated at the pizza house when the model strolled in. All eyes turned to gaze at her, and Stevie had to admit that, in her skin-tight jeans and loose frilly shirt, Irena looked delectable. Anthony beckoned her towards them.

After a brief glance at them both and a mute question to Anthony, Irena offered her face to be kissed. She said a shy hello to Stevie, and they made random conversation as they waited for the food to arrive. With an attempt to contain her emotions which inevitably led in the direction of jealousy, Stevie complimented Irena on the last lot of prints she had seen. In turn, the model asked Stevie about the Scottish assignment. Stevie answered as best she could.

'But James must have told you all about it,' Anthony manoeuvred the conversation on to the ground he wanted to investigate.

'He wasn't very communicative when I saw him last night,' Irena offered.

So James was spending his nights with Irena, Stevie thought, her heart sinking even further.

The model looked at her reflectively. 'I thought he was having a thing with you,' she said candidly to Stevie, 'and I was very jealous. But now . . .' she threw a loving look at Anthony.

Stevie looked at her plate.

'I guess I was wrong,' Irena returned her eyes to Stevie and shrugged. 'James is in far too foul a temper to be engaged on any new affair. He's a passionate man.'

The way she brought out the phrase made Stevie's pulse race with remembrance.

Anthony interrupted. 'James has left the agency. Did he tell you why?'

Irena looked surprised and then shook her head slowly. 'No, he spent the whole time grilling me, as you say, about a model called Marissa Carr. I don't know her, so all I could tell him was that she has a good reputation, is known to be co-operative. Perhaps he wants to use her and she's tied to a rival firm?'

Anthony turned a questioning look at Stevie, who gazed at them both with a mounting sense of bewilderment. She finished as much as she could swallow of her pizza and excused herself.

'I'll join you in a little while, Stevie.' Anthony called after her.

She nodded and walked desultorily back to the office. Anthony returned only moments after her.

'Do you think James might have had an unhappy affair with Marissa and not realised she was your sister?' was the first thing he said to her.

'No,' Stevie looked shocked. 'Marissa would have told me. She's not cagey about these things.'

'Well, I don't know, Stevie,' he shook his head. 'It's all very odd. You've been working so hard for him.'

Stevie felt the tears welling up in her eyes, as they so often had over the last few days. 'I think I'll take the rest of the day off,' she mumbled. 'I'm not much use at the moment.'

Anthony patted her on the shoulder and shooed her off. 'We'll get to the bottom of this yet,' he said consolingly. 'No man would give *you* up just like that,' he snapped his fingers.

Stevie wanted to say that James, from what she could deduce, had given even Irena up 'just like that', but she kept her thoughts to herself. Lying on the sofa that afternoon, she thought the whole thing through again and again. A small suspicion began to dawn in her mind and by the time Marissa came home that evening, it had taken on enormous proportions. As lightly as she could, she said to Marissa in the midst of dinner, 'I had lunch with Irena Borg today and she mentioned your name in connection with a man called Alastair Reid.'

Marissa shrugged. 'A long time ago, all that. Not a very happy event in my life. He was a boy, really, Alastair. He kept ringing me, pursuing me, and then suddenly he died—in a car crash, I think,' she fumbled in her bag for one of her rare cigarettes. 'Strange,' she looked at Stevie quizzically, 'I don't remember Irena Borg in that circle.'

Stevie waffled something and kept her face as controlled as she could. Then, pleading exhaustion, she went off to bed. A feeling of impotent rage overwhelmed her. It was closely followed by a sense of utter hopelessness. She had been trapped by an absurd fate into a situation over which she had no power. Of

all the models in the world, it would have to be her
sister for whom James's brother had raced to his death.
There was nothing she could do about it, nothing she
could say to James which would annihilate her
association with Marissa and his brother's tragedy.

The next day, she woke with her mind made up. She
wrapped the emerald ring—kept by her bedside for
days—in a little packet and sent it off to James,
recorded delivery. Then she went directly to see Mr
Brewster and announced that she was resigning: she
was homesick for America, she explained, and was
going back. He protested, insisting that it was only a
passing phase. She was tired; the Reid business was
something of a shock. When Stevie brushed aside his
words, he said he would grant her a leave of absence to
think the matter over. He wanted her with the firm. To
ease things along, she promised that she would let him
know definitely in a month's time.

Back in her own office, she packed her few
belongings and told Anthony of her resolve, forestalling
his questions by saying it was only a leave of absence.
Then with a promise to write soon, she marched out of
the office. Jan, at reception, stopped her. 'Another of
your admirers on the telephone,' she announced
provocatively.

Stevie's heart began to race. Perhaps it was James—
James at last! Her face fell when she heard Jordan's
voice. She had all but forgotten he was still in England.

'Stevie, I've only got another few nights. Can I see
you?'

'All you like, Jordan. I'm coming home,' Stevie said
flatly, unable to draw up the energy to explain that her
decision had nothing to do with him.

There was a breathless pause at the other end of the
line, followed by a low whistle. 'Shall we fly together,
Stevie? I'm due to leave on Saturday morning.'

'That sounds fine,' Stevie said dully. 'I'll make the
arrangements. It will probably be simplest to meet at

the airport on the day. I have a lot of loose ends to tie up.' She rang off.

Explaining her decision to Marissa proved more difficult than Stevie had foreseen.

'You can't just go and bury yourself in a small town for the rest of your life because of one unhappy love affair,' her sister pleaded reasonably.

'Just watch me!' Stevie tried to joke amidst tears.

'That bastard!' Marissa hugged her. 'I'm going to make his name mud!'

'No,' Stevie protested, 'just leave it be, Marissa.'

'You really love him, don't you, despite the way he's treated you?' Marissa looked at her wonderingly.

Stevie was only able to nod as the tears streamed down her face and she thought of how she had been raised to the heights of bliss, only to be flung down into the depths of despair.

CHAPTER TEN

STEVIE drove mutely through the small New England town, trying to let its once familiar contours obliterate the recent past: the white clapperboard residences, set well back from the road, the simple church with its single steeple looking as if it should house a weathervane, and finally the bus depot with its quiet unruffled air, so different from the noisy, sprawling New York station where she had boarded the Greyhound.

Murmuring an excuse-me to the youth sitting next to her, she slipped off the bus and waited for the driver to unload her large case. Then, having checked it at the luggage counter, with a promise that she would be back to collect it later, she walked slowly homewards.

She felt strangely disembodied, as if she were floating in some alien space, quite distinct from her arms and legs. Jet-lag, she told herself crossly, barring her mind from searching out other reasons. She had spent a sleepless night in a dingy New York hotel close to the bus station, after having bidden Jordan goodbye at Kennedy Airport. It had taken her a little time to convince him that he shouldn't break his promise to visit his father—who now lived in Washington—for her sake. She would be at home and they would meet soon enough. 'But, Jordan,' she had pleaded, had *insisted*, 'I haven't come home for you. What I said the other night stands. We're friends, that's all. Good friends, I hope.'

Jordan had pooh-poohed her comments aside and reached for her hand. Stevie had let it lie there, like some foreign object. She didn't have the strength to protest. All her energy had been sapped in trying to

173

make sense of her feelings. But at last Jordan had gone off, and now, as she turned the key in the lock and stepped into the cool airy interior of her childhood home, she concentrated on putting London, James, the whole experience out of her mind.

She looked round the comfortable drawing room with its well-worn chairs, the dining table adorned with a large pot of flowers bearing a message from her father, the kitchen with its row of homemade jam jars prepared by the housekeeper Mrs Seaton, who had been with them ever since Stevie could remember. Yes, despite everything, it was still home. She went up to her room. It was just as she had left it—the blue, flowered quilt, the small desk, the shelves piled high with books she had never wanted to part with.

Stevie flung herself down on the bed and for the first time since she had fully realised that James was now for ever gone from her life, she let the sobs shake her violently, giving way like a child to unrestrained misery. It was finally the hopelessness of it all that had beaten her. A small part of herself was angry with James for letting his own past control him to such an extent. But she knew that there was nothing she could do. Their love—if it was that, she thought bitterly—was too young, too vulnerable to stand in the face of the past and obliterate it. She remembered again and again the pain in James's face when he had first told her about Alastair, his anger at himself, his contempt and rage for the woman he felt was partially responsible for his brother's death. My sister, Stevie repeated to herself miserably for the hundredth time.

'Stevie, Stevie, I'm home!' Her father's voice woke her from a numbed sleep, and she rubbed her eyes open just as his tall distinguished form appeared through the door of her room.

'Hello, sweetie.' He sat down on the bed and cradled her in his arms. 'Your mother tells me you've been having a rough time.'

Stevie stiffened and then relaxed as she looked into his kindly, worried face.

'Oh, it's nothing. I'll be all right, now that I'm home again.'

'I have very distinct orders not to let you sulk, to make sure you get plenty of fresh air and rest—and,' he paused, 'to take you back to London with me, even if I have to drag you by the hair.'

'Oh, Dad, what's Mother been telling you?'

'Simply that you've done very well and that you've exhausted yourself.' He avoided her eyes. 'Now run along and make yourself beautiful for dinner while I go and fetch your case. Mrs Seaton has cooked your favourite stew and I've invited some friends over to keep us company.'

Stevie was about to protest and tell her father that she didn't want to see anyone, but one look at his face told her it would be easier simply to let things be.

She showered, changed into one of the many pairs of jeans which she had left behind in her closet and a white tee-shirt. As she looked at herself in the mirror which had reflected her face for so many years, she realised that despite the fact that she was thinner, despite the shadows beneath her eyes, she looked absurdly young. Not at all like a person whose life is over, she said to herself determinedly: while another voice grumbled that appearances were deceiving.

The days passed in a kind of numbed impassivity. Stevie dragged herself round the house listlessly or lay about in the garden rereading old books in which all the heroes took on James's proportions. She watched her skin turn brown in the sun. When her father was home, she made an effort to act cheerful. It was the nights which were more difficult as James's image rampantly pervaded Stevie's dreams, his physical presence at once so real, so tangible, that she could feel his kisses on her lips, her skin, rousing her into a waking which could only be a brutal affirmation of his absence.

Jordan returned and began to be a constant dinner guest. Seeing him in this familiar space, on his own home ground, Stevie wondered whether it would perhaps be best simply to acquiesce to him, to settle back on to the old footing. It would at least be some kind of a life and perhaps, in time, she would grow to love him. But her heart sank at the thought and her skin grew cold, clammy.

No, she must be honest with herself and fair to Jordan. She didn't love him as, despite herself, she still loved James. And she could never explain to him what it meant to have felt something far greater, something overpowering, for another man. She would be living out a constant betrayal of them both. She looked at Jordan across the table, his youthful face which seemed somehow shadowy, unformed, and in her mind's eye she saw the chiselled granite of James's features. The pit widened in her stomach. Would she ever be able to forget him?

'A penny for your thoughts,' her father broke into her reverie.

'I was just thinking how nice it would be to go for a walk by the lake tomorrow,' said Stevie, fumbling for ideas.

'Let's do just that,' Jordan offered instantly.

'O.K,' Stevie agreed, rising from the dinner table and promising herself that she would use that opportunity to talk to Jordan again. She had been avoiding seeing him alone. It was childish, she scolded herself.

In the small hours of that night, a plan began to jell in her mind. She wouldn't, she couldn't go back to London and the physical proximity of all those memories, when her father travelled there. His constant references to the imminent trip always brought her heart to her mouth and the sting of tears to her eyes. No, when her father left, she would take herself off and go to New York. There she would find a job and start her life afresh. Resigned, like one of those puritan heroines, she added to herself, who know they have lost the most important part of their lives but carry on all the same. The thought didn't bring her the comfort it once might have.

On Saturday afternoon Jordan came to pick her up and they strolled down the path which after many twists and turns led to the lake. Jordan broke into Stevie's chit-chat before she was ready to begin on more serious subjects.

'Stevie, I'm not an idiot—I know you've been avoiding seeing me alone. I've read and re-read your letter and, given that you're back here, I can't see that any of it makes any difference to us, really.'

Stevie couldn't bring herself to answer directly. They were now by the lakeside and they sat down on a familiar patch. She looked into the water's rippling blue and was suddenly reminded of the stream she had swum in with James. She shivered. Jordan's words intruded on her with a hostile persistence. 'In your letter you talked of another man who'd helped you see what love was all about. But presumably that's over now, since you're here.'

Stevie nodded, unable to trust her voice.

'Well, if going to bed with him helped you to *see*, then perhaps the same performance with me might have a similar result,' he said bitterly, and with unusual aggression, pulled her roughly to him. 'Let's find out if you've at least learned to kiss now, Stevie,' and he forced his lips on hers with clumsy menace.

With a struggle, Stevie jumped up and ran along the water's edge. Jordan was right behind her. She stopped abruptly and turned to face him. There was no point in running away and she guessed she deserved at least some of Jordan's resentment, even contempt. But if nothing else, his touch had proved to her once and for all that she couldn't be his.

'Stop it Jordan—I don't feel that way about you. I know I've behaved badly, childishly. But now, if you can see your way to it,' she met his eyes with forceful insistence, 'I'd like us to be friends. It's not so paltry a thing.' She hesitated and then added with a savage note, 'It seems to last longer than the other, in any case.'

Jordan didn't respond, but he kept pace with her, as she began to walk up the hill. Finally he spoke. 'OK, Stevie, you win. We'll be friends.' He put his hand out to her and she took it. 'I think you're probably right in any case. It just took me a long time to see it, assimilate it.' They looked at each other for a moment and then began to stroll side by side, talking more easily with each step. By the time they reached the house, Stevie had learned, with a mixture of relief and a passing unease, of Jordan's interest in a new lab assistant. There goes the last bit of my safety net, she thought to herself wryly, while out loud she told Jordan how much she would like to meet the woman.

She invited Jordan in for coffee and they sat together in the living room and listened quietly to music. Suddenly the doorbell interrupted a delicate melody. 'Dad must have forgotten his key.' Stevie got to her feet. 'You're getting absentminded in your old age, Dad!' she called as she opened the door. Her heart lurched and the colour drained out of her face. 'James!' The name emerged from her lips with a strangled gasp.

He stood tall on the threshold, his powerful body clad in the cream summer suit she remembered so well, his face ruggedly handsome in the late afternoon light. His eyes searched her face, straying pensively over her lips.

'Will you invite me in, Stevie?' he asked, his voice low, each word echoing in her ears like the dialogue of a distant dream.

Stevie stepped aside for him to enter, not daring to speak, so violent had the throbbing of her pusle become.

'Who is it, Stevie?' Jordan was suddenly beside them, and she forced her thick tongue into speech.

'You remember each other, I think,' she said to them both.

The two men eyed each other suspiciously, charging the atmosphere in the room with a palpable tension. Somehow Stevie managed to serve some coffee, to make the pretence of conversation. Half of her wished Jordan would leave, while part of her wanted him to stay until she could collect a little of her senses.

James was not so patient. Just as Jordan was about to pour himself a second cup of coffee, he intervened abruptly. 'I'm sorry to intrude on you two, but Stevie and I have some urgent business to discuss,' he said with customary authority.

Looking to Stevie, who briefly nodded agreement, Jordan rose to go, but not without first kissing her on the cheek and saying a possessive, 'I'll see you later, Stevie.'

For some reason, this little gesture gave her strength. She turned defiantly to James. 'What urgent business could we possibly have to discuss?'

'Forgotten so soon?' He looked at her mockingly, and suddenly he was next to her, pulling her to him, his lips crushing her mouth with a pent-up urgency that took her breath away and brought a tingle of awareness to every part of her skin. The familiar smell of his maleness enveloped her, and it was only with an enormous effort that she managed to draw away from him.

'I'm not some shuttlecock to be bandied about by your whims!' she began angrily.

James put a finger to her lips. 'Quiet, Ms Henderson,' he ordered. 'I know I have a great deal of explaining to do, so just sit there and listen.'

Stevie bridled at his tone, but one look at his eyes, intently dark under the furrowed brow, kept her still.

He reached in his jacket pocket. 'First of all, there's this bit of urgent business.' He took the emerald from the box she had wrapped it in and reached for her hand. 'I haven't accepted it back, you know.'

She tried to withdraw her hand, but he gripped it fiercely and slipped the ring on to her finger.

She laughed shrilly, 'For services rendered!' The bitterness of her tone made his jaw tense.

'Hush!' There was a fierce glitter in his eyes. 'Marissa came to see me a few days ago,' he began in a low tone, 'simply came to the door with no warning. She started abusing me, calling me a first class fool, a swine.'

Stevie gasped.

James chuckled hoarsely. 'I had no choice but to invite her in. The neighbours might have agreed with me that it was an accurate assessment.'

For the first time, Stevie noticed that his face looked haggard, that there were shadowy hollows beneath his eyes.

'She continued to illuminate me about my sterling virtues,' James smiled in self-mockery, 'and finished by telling me that if I was making her wonderful sister pay for the fact that I thought that she, Marissa, had killed my soppy idiot of a brother, then I was not only the world's prize bastard, but stupidly immoral to boot. Or something like that.' A droll expression played over his face. 'She talks as much as you do, this sister of yours.'

Stevie suddenly laughed as she imagined the juicy epithets which would have come to Marissa's lips. Then she looked at James intently, challenging him to defy her, 'Marissa is wonderful,' she breathed.

'What else could she be? She's your sister.' He smiled at her warmly as she gazed at him in surprise. 'What I want to know is how she, how you, put two and two together.'

Stevie explained in a cool voice. 'The penny dropped after Irena told me you'd been asking questions about Marissa, and I asked Marissa whether she'd ever met an Alastair Reid. But I never said anything to her about the connection with you,' Stevie added defensively. 'She must have worked that out for herself.'

James laughed, 'Thank God for Irena and for the

London web! I never thought I'd be grateful for it.'

'Grateful?' Stevie looked at him suspiciously.

'Yes, Stevie. More grateful than I can say.' He looked at her gravely, his eyes raking over her as he reached for her hand and squeezed it as if he would never let it go. 'Don't you know that?' She shook her head and he groaned comically, 'I see I'm going to have to get down on my knees!'

'You most certainly are,' she retorted savagely. A bright wild spirit suddenly invaded her after weeks of lethargy. 'And while you're down there, I shall kick you very hard!'

He groaned again and then abruptly stood to his full height, towering over her threateningly. 'I refuse to be kicked in your father's house.' His eyes smiling again, he pulled her up to him and kissed her lightly, deliciously on the lips. 'Now, you have five minutes to change into your most seductive dress and then I'm going to take you out for a sumptuous dinner. After which I solemnly promise to get down on my knees.'

With a smile hovering over her lips, Stevie went up to her room. Carefully she put on one of her London dresses, a white full-skirted embroidered cotton with a little camisole top. She was pleased now that all her lying about in the garden had brought a warm bronze glow to her skin. The eyes that looked at her from the mirror seemed to have been transformed into emerald radiance. She brushed her hair gaily, bringing out its sheen, treated herself to a little perfume and then bounced downstairs. Only for a fleeting moment did she pause to wonder at how quickly she was once again enmeshed in James's magic.

She found James deep in conversation with her father and she eyed the two men suspiciously. Her father's eyes twinkled over her. 'You look very pretty, my dear. It's good to see you in a dress again!'

Stevie flushed, her embarrassment not lessened by the lazy caress of James's eyes.

'James and I have been getting to know each other a little.' Stevie was amazed at how quickly the two men had reached a first name basis. It made her even more suspicious.

With a little smile on his lips, her father continued, 'He's just invited me to a wedding in Scotland, invited me to give the bride away, in fact. I said I'd be perfectly willing, as long as she was.'

Stevie's mouth dropped in amazement. 'But I haven't . . .'

Her father cut her off. 'I shall leave the two of you alone to discuss it. I have some work to do.' But before he reached the door, he turned back and added, his eyes still twinkling, 'From what Marissa told me over the phone yesterday, Stevie, you'll be in good hands.' Then, waving a brief goodbye, he made his way towards his study.

Stevie looked at James defiantly. 'I haven't said yes to anything yet. You behaved abominably!' She was suddenly irritated by his arrogance which assumed he could have her with a single snap of his fingers.

'I know, I know,' James gestured comically. 'The knees. But I promised you dinner first.' He trailed an arm casually round her waist, stroking the curve of her hips with his fingertips, and Stevie's skin melted in response. He looked at her mischievously, 'Are you sure you haven't said yes to *anything* yet?'

She pulled away from him. 'There's more to life than that—than your touching me,' she said contemptuously.

He confronted her with the full force of his gaze. 'I know, Stevie, much more. That's why I'm here.' Suddenly he laughed, and a devilish light sparkled in his eyes, 'Come and see what's waiting outside. It's a tiny part of the "more".'

Parked in front of the house was a white Thunderbird convertible, its hood down. 'The lady's chariot awaits, straight from John F. Kennedy's rent-a-car service.'

Stevie made no response to his playful humour and he drove swiftly over the hilly country roads. He seemed to know his exact destination. 'I stumbled on to a wonderful hotel on my way here,' he explained. 'They promised superb seafood.'

Stevie continued to look disgruntled. She had the distinct sense that everyone was plotting around her. James shot her a pleading glance, 'Stevie, please, smile at me, even if I am, in your sister's words, a prize bastard.'

'As long as you remember that it commits me to nothing,' she said emphatically, 'that I never committed myself to anything.'

He swerved the car dangerously round a bend. His fingers were whitely tense on the steering wheel. 'I see,' he said grimly, adding after a moment, 'You still haven't decided against Jordan, you mean?'

'You haven't exactly given me much to decide *for*,' Stevie said hotly, the anger and misery of weeks evident in the bitterness of her tone.

He screeched the car to a halt in front of an old white clapperboard hotel, nestling gently in a wood of maples and scented pine. Gripping her arm fiercely, he guided her through the door. Stevie could feel his fingers imprinting themselves on her skin. It was only when they were settled at either side of a small table covered with a starched white tablecloth and glistening silver cutlery that he spoke again.

'That evening in London when I last saw you,' he searched her eyes before downing a half-full glass of wine, 'I thought you wanted me, wanted to marry me,' he slurred the words. 'Though I must say Jordan's presence did disconcert me somewhat.'

Stevie shrugged, 'A lot of women have wanted you. It hasn't made much difference. Take Irena for one, and the way you've treated her.'

He gazed at her in astonishment. 'What do you know about that?' His voice was impatient.

'Only that having had your fill of her, you threw her aside,' she brought out coldly.

His eyes blazed into her. 'That, Stevie, is absolute nonsense! When I first met Irena in Stockholm, she was in a terrible state. She'd stopped modelling, she'd been doing too many drugs. I tried to pull her out of it—successfully, I might add; urged her back to work. If in the process she mistook me for a saviour, talked herself into the idea that she was in love with me,' he shrugged, 'there's little I can do about that. In any case, Stevie,' he looked at her now with indolent mockery, 'I never suggested to you that I was as pure as the driven snow.'

She lowered her eyes away from him, unable to bear the probing force of his, and tried to sip the cold clam chowder she usually loved.

'Stevie,' James's voice was suddenly mellow, 'I didn't for one minute mean to hurt you. I've been more careful with you, more patient, than with any woman I can remember. It's just that when I realised Marissa was your sister, the world started to crumble. I couldn't make sense of anything. The woman I love, sister to the woman who had been in some way responsible for my brother's death . . . It's not an easy fact to assimilate.'

Stevie's heart skipped a beat. She had distinctly heard him say he loved her. She looked into the blue of his eyes wonderingly and then stopped herself before all reason left her. 'But Marissa wasn't responsible, you know,' she said, looking down at his hands.

'I know, I know,' he spoke as if his impatience with himself had reached a point of exasperation. 'But I'd built up this myth of a cold, wicked ice-goddess who'd murdered my brother with my collusion. And his death wasn't somehow so distinct from the other deaths I'd witnessed,' he added simply. 'They all seemed to blur together into that one personal death.' He searched her eyes gravely.

Stevie looked at the lines of pain etched on his face,

remembered the story about his journalist friend, and instinctively her hand went out to grasp his.

He held her eyes to his. 'I knew I should ring you, speak to you, explain, but I couldn't. I just lay about, gripped in paralytic guilt, knowing, of course, that Alastair's death was in no way Marissa's fault, that the fact that I wanted you was in no way related to any of it, but unable to do anything about it all—unable, as well, to confront you with my own despair. A kind of shell-shock, I guess.'

He stroked her hand softly, weaving soft circles of sensation in her skin.

'Then, when Marissa arrived and started abusing me, it was like that proverbial slap in the face that wakens you. It did me a world of good. I started thinking about you rather than brooding about the past.' He looked at Stevie, his eyes smouldering in the granite-hard face. 'I realised,' his voice caught, 'realised how very precious you were to me.'

She looked up at him shyly, a smile lighting her face, 'That's enough now, or you'll have me crying for you!'

'And we wouldn't want that before I'd got down on my knees,' he matched her tone. 'Eat your lobster, Stevie. I don't want you thin enough to model,' he grumbled menacingly.

She bit into her food, tasting it for the first time in weeks, relishing every mouthful, despite the sense of his eyes on her, following her every gesture. But before she had finished, he stopped her. 'That's enough now.'

She looked at his plate, noticing that he had barely touched it, and eyed him questioningly. In response he took her arm and guided her up the stairs towards his room. He closed the door firmly behind them. 'I want to be alone with you, Stevie, away from all those faces.' His eyes lingered on her and then slowly he traced the shape of her face with his fingers, her eyes, her cheeks her nose and then, with a featherlight touch, her lips. Gently then he drew her to him, claiming her lips in a

kiss that mounted in passion as her arms flew around
him, gripping him with her own stored hunger.

'Oh, Stevie, say you'll have me,' he murmured into
her ear.

She shook her head away from him, and he caught it
in a vicelike grip. 'Why? I don't care about Jordan,
don't care about anything or anyone else. I'll make you
forget Jordan, make you forget any pain I've caused
you.' His eyes burned into her, raking her body with a
smouldering insolence. Ruthlessly he devoured her
mouth, his savage ferocity sending the blood clamouring
through her veins, making her pulse-beat palpable to
him, opening a void in the depths of her which only he
could fill. She cleaved to him and suddenly he lifted her
in his arms and carried her towards the bed. 'I'll make
you say yes, Stevie.'

She looked into his face, her eyes languorous as they
gazed into his. 'Knees,' she mouthed to him, and he
groaned, depositing her gently on the plush bedcover.
Then, with exaggerated grace, he knelt in front of her,
took her hands and kissed her fingers, nipping each
with tender little bites in the process.

'Ms Stevie Henderson, I do hereby solemnly and
seriously and in the pitch of desire ask you to be my
lawfully wedded wife, to have and to hold—and don't
you dare say no!'

Stevie shook her head and looked at him wickedly.

'Why not, Stevie?' The pain in his eyes was palpable.
'I love you, you silly fool!' he roared.

'At last!' she gasped theatrically, and grasping her
hands to her breast, she addressed an invisible audience.
'I thought he'd never say it to my face!' Then she pulled
him to her, running her fingers through the rough
thickness of his hair, covering every inch of his face
with kisses.

'I told you we Scots were secretive,' he drawled,
pressing her to him in a caress that stirred all the
intimate places of her body. Stevie moaned as he trailed

fire against her throat. She clung to him in the joy of pure arousal, her flesh burning against his firmness, her hands seeking out the satin of his skin, the rougher texture of his chest, the taut muscles of his shoulders. A provocative little imp in her suddenly found a voice. 'When did you first want me, James?'

He rested his head on one arm, while his eyes roamed over her body. A hoarse chuckle escaped him. 'Eons ago—when you first called me Genghis Khan. There's a spirited woman, I thought to myself, a sensible woman, who understands the measure of things. I'll have to tame that one.' He looked at her rakishly.

'Genghis Khan!' Stevie teased, and then her eyes widened into seriousness. 'But when did you decide you wanted me *for good*?' she emphasised.

'When I proposed to you, you wretch, in the car on the way to Scotland. I'd been scheming—don't tell me you didn't realise?' He looked at her in mock astonishment. 'Embroiling you as my assistant, kidnapping you away with me so you'd forget that Jordan of yours, not to mention that coxcomb of a Brewster who seemed to be everywhere with you.' His eyes grew mellow as she stroked his hair. 'But when I actually said the words, "my wife-to-be" it all jelled. I knew that Mother was an excuse. I wanted you—wanted you for good. I'm sorry the ghosts intervened, but it will be all right now, darling. I'll make it up to you.'

His eyes searched her face, framed against the pillow by the golden fire of her hair. 'And you, my pure little puritan ... for you are, aren't you, or I wouldn't have been patient for so long?'—she nodded shyly, in response to his question and he chuckled lovingly—'when did you at last acknowledge to yourself that you wanted me?'

Stevie's impish side took over. 'I haven't yet.' She let her eyes skim his body provocatively.

With a hoarse groan James was upon her, his hands stirring her body into life, awakening the skin of her limbs, her breasts, so that she arched against him in an ecstasy of sense and surrendered her mouth to his in a drowning kiss.

'Stevie,' his voice husky with emotion, carried over the pounding of her blood, and suddenly his eyes were upon her, proud as a panther's, 'you haven't answered my question yet. Will you? Marry me? Love me?'

'Yes,' she breathed into his skin, his lips, his ears. 'Yes, my love, yes! I've been saying it to myself for light years,' and with an urgency as great as his, she gave herself up to the pure white flame that consumed them both.

How to join in a whole new world of romance

It's very easy to subscribe to the Mills & Boon Reader Service. As a regular reader, you can enjoy a whole range of special benefits. Bargain offers. Big cash savings. Your own free Reader Service newsletter, packed with knitting patterns, recipes, competitions, and exclusive book offers.

We send you the very latest titles each month, postage and packing free – no hidden extra charges. There's absolutely no commitment – you receive books for only as long as you want.

We'll send you details. Simply send the coupon – or drop us a line for details about the Mills & Boon Reader Service Subscription Scheme.
Post to: Mills & Boon Reader Service, P.O. Box 236, Thornton Road, Croydon, Surrey CR9 3RU, England.
*Please note: READERS IN SOUTH AFRICA please write to: Mills & Boon Reader Service of Southern Africa, Private Bag X3010, Randburg 2125, S. Africa.

Please send me details of the Mills & Boon Subscription Scheme.
NAME (Mrs/Miss) _____ EP3
ADDRESS _____

COUNTY/COUNTRY_____ POST/ZIP CODE_____
BLOCK LETTERS, PLEASE

Mills & Boon
the rose of romance